S'mores. More Adventures at Camp Sedation Falls

Veronica Krug

S'MORES. MORE ADVENTURES AT CAMP SEDATION FALLS

1

S' mores
      More Adventures at Camp Sedation Falls
   By Veronica Krug
   Copyright @ 2024

Introduction

2

I'm retired now...from camp counseling, camp director, director of litter control, selling Bob Evans sausage from a mall kiosk, sorting mail, and teaching middle school students.

For the years that I was working and raising two children, I would spend every spare minute of free time writing stories. Stories have always been my escape from the trials of everyday life. It's like having the best dream ever and being able to retell it in vivid detail.

Ask my family, and they will tell you I'm a great storyteller, or was it lier?...in any case, I came up with some doozies; like the time I skipped school and told my teacher I didn't have an excuse because my mother fell and broke her leg. Who should show up at our home with a casserole for my poor crippled mother? You got it. That dang teacher! Woo, was my rear sore.

Summer recreation was my favorite job. I got to play along with the children every day, plan fun field trips, listen, and watch their reactions to the first time trying new things. I was told I should be a teacher. The pay is a lot better and I could have summers off. Well, I worked extra jobs to help pay for my tuition and I was considered an "older than average" student. After graduating,

I was hired to teach inner city middle school and BAM, culture shock. The shock was that I had to WORK, and so did the kids. It was hard inspiring them, though I tried and at times got into trouble for it; like the time I rode a skateboard into class to teach design. It's a tough period for that age. I imagine everyone reading this remembers being bullied at least once, and it was in middle school. They are testing life, testing boundaries, and testing their parents.

But, middle school children are fun when you really observe them, and listen. I taught in that city for 23 years, and retired when I became an "older than average teacher".

I was inspired to write this series when I saw a need for senior citizens to get a break from the challenges of getting older, just like the children. To me, Camp Sedation Falls is a place where they can have non-judgmental fun. Pure fun, like when they were young and had few responsibilities. Retirement is a new chapter in life. One I looked forward to and enjoy because I now have time to write about my best dreams ever in vivid detail.

There is no actual Sedation Falls, but wouldn't it be fun if there was? Enjoy book 2 of the continued camp adventures.

To everyone who wanted more of the story.

"I'm gonna live 'til the livin' runs out."

--Walter

"You know you're getting old when you stoop to tie your shoelaces and wonder what else you could do down there."

--George Burns

"You don't stop laughing when you grow old, you grow old when you stop laughing."

--George Bernard Shaw

"Old age is an excellent time for outrage. My goal is to say or do at least one outrageous thing every week."

--Maggie Kuhn

3

A NEW SEASON

"Dag nab it, not agin, Mildred!" Walter, a recent partner with Camp Sedation Falls, pulls and pushes against the jammed bathroom stall door. "Why didn't you use the damn new one in yer cabin?"

Mildred's voice, shaky and nearly gone from calling for help, whispers under the bottom of the door. "This one was closer."

Tyronne, AKA Stitch, bursts onto the scene. His smile and bright teeth remind Walter of the Chesire cat. He grips an electric drill in one hand—the gun to save the day. He raises a stiff arm between Walter and the door. A cartoonish smug curls one lip. "Step aside...I gots this." Stitch takes the cord with his free hand. "Where's the outlet?"

Walter crosses his arms. "There ain't one, idjet."

Stitch places the drill onto the counter raising a finger. "Plan B."

"Hello?" Mildred calls.

"Don't worry, Miss Mildred, I got ya." Stitch reaches a hand to the back of his pants and brings out a screwdriver. He takes ahold of the stall handle and gingerly jiggles it. Walter steps back, avoiding any accidental poke in the eye as Stitch, a doctor performing delicate surgery, removes each screw from the post holding the door. Stitch tries to lift the door, but it's too heavy. He bows to Walter.

"Fer cryin' out..." Walter steps in front of the door and with an "Oomph" lifts it from the hinges and places it against a wall.

Mildred stands in the now open stall. Her yellow blouse partly tucked into her purple capris, hands thrust to her hips. "If you had properly maintained this place, it wouldn't have happened. I could have expired in there."

Walter eyes her up and down. "Looks to me I was too late."

She raises a hand to slap him. "Why you old..."

"If I had a heart attack boostin' this damn door, it woulda been yer fault."

Stitch steps between them, turning to Mildred. "I'm so sorry, Ma'am, but it was my fault. I'm the camp maintenance man now."

"I know that honey, but old Walter here should be up on these things. It happened before."

Walter peeks over Stitch's shoulder. "No, you locked yerself in the whole damn bathhouse last year. So, I build you new toilets in yer blasted cabins this year, an' you still gotta come down here an' give me shit."

Mildred storms out of the stall to wash her hands in the sink, her voice suddenly back. "I'm telling Richard Darling Senior about this!"

"Be my guest, go tell Richard Darling Senior." he waves while turning his back to her. "How'd I git myself into this mess anyways." Walter mumbles.

Stitch gathers his tools. "Dude, that ain't nothin'. This is just the beginning. We ain't even open yet."

Walter scratches his head in thought. "Yer right, where the hell did she come from?" He rushes to the door, eyes searching. "An' where did she go?"

"She's s'posed to be a Carin' Souls resident."

"Have you seen her 'round here afore today?"

"Not since last year, sir."

Walter marches out the door. "If those assholes up the hill dropped their folks off two weeks early, I'm gonna tan their hides."

Stitch's shoulders square and he grips the drill like a gun. "You got that right."

"Go check out the cabins." Walter marches to the office he shares with Richard Darling Senior.

***

Richard Darling Senior is sitting at the desk previously occupied by his son, Junior, who is now a manager at Caring Souls Adult Center a mile up the hill from Camp Sedation Falls, spitting distance from the Blue Ridge Mountains in North Carolina. Senior bought the camp at auction with his old friend, Dingo, a year ago. It was an abandoned Boy Scout retreat with an empty pool, a bathhouse in need of serious plumbing repairs, a weed infested lake surrounded by eight rustic cabins with leaky roofs, and a large mess hall with a kitchen in the back a bear had ravaged. Senior believed Junior would manage the camp and all he had to worry about was take in the profit; instead, it was all outgo, and they would have lost the camp if it wasn't for Walter Evans investing his life savings into it. The place is looking much better now, and there are bathrooms in each cabin thanks to Walter. He owes a lot to that crotchety, generous man.

Senior pulls open a drawer to an array of papers, candy wrappers, bottle tops, rubber bands, and something sticky and brown in the front right corner. He throws his arms up in dismay. "What the...where's the damn contracts?" He opens a side drawer to what appears to be files. "Whew, thank you." He shuffles through them. The file sleeves are empty. Behind them is a huge stack of paperwork. "Gah!" He lifts the papers from the drawer with both hands and plops them on top of the desk. "That boy is gonna..."

Walter barges into the office. His thick mustache twitching like an electrocuted wooly bear. "Kid, we got a problem."

Senior continues to flick through the papers. "Yes, we do."

"Mildred got stuck in the bathhouse again."

"Uh, huh."

"She shouldn't be here. The idjets dropped the old folks from Caring Souls here already. We got to find 'em."

"Uh, huh, I'm looking." *Shuffle, shuffle.*

"Fer what?"

Senior lifts his head, blinking. "What?"

"Jesus Cripes." Walter stomps to his desk on the other side of the room. "I need a drink." He pulls open a side drawer and lifts a bottle of Jim Beam from it, twists off the cap, and chugs from the bottle.

Senior looks like an apologetic constipated mutt. "I'm sorry, but have you seen the camper contracts?"

Walter puts the bottle down with a thud and points to a pile of papers in front of him. "Bub, they're right here."

Senior relaxes. "Oh, thank God. I don't even know what this mess is all about. No wonder we almost lost this place. I'm going to have words with my son."

"No, yer not."

Senior raises his brows in surprise. "Excuse me?"

"You teach that boy how to organize yer shit? No. it's on you, Kemosabe. We ain't born automatically knowin' everythin'...'cept fer me." The mustache curls into a wide smile.

Senior reaches out with one hand, grinning. "Can I have some of that?"

"Come an' git it." Walter holds out his whiskey as Senior walks over to take it. He wipes the lip of the bottle with the sleeve of his shirt, then drinks.

Walter's eyes narrow at Senior. "Dumbass, whiskey kills germs."

Senior shivers after the warm intense liquor slips down his throat. Doing his best to breathe, he wheezes, "You're right. What do we have to find?"

"Mildred. She's here somewhere. Caring Souls must be here."

"But camp is two weeks away. Junior knows that."

Walter taps the side of his head with a finger. "Duh. Stitch is lookin' fer 'em."

BEEP, BEEP! A car horn blares into their conversation. An old, filthy pickup truck speeds up the drive. Walter and Senior step out onto the porch of the dining hall. The truck slides on the gravel to a stop in front of them. A man with shoulder length silky brown hair steps out of the driver's side wearing aviator sunglasses, a Hawaiian shirt and baggy cargo shorts. His skinny legs are a stark contrast to the bulk of his stomach.

Senior recognizes him immediately. "Dingo?" A knot forms in his stomach. He counted on Dingo to be his partner when they bought the camp. The man destroyed that trust.

Dingo waves and trots to the passenger side. He helps a petite woman with purple hair cut to the bottom of her earlobes out of the truck. She's wearing a pink shift dress looking more like a night gown to Senior.

She waves. "You Hoo!"

"Miss Wren." Senior isn't sure if he should be happy to see them or pissed off. Dingo used him, spent his money on a business venture in Las Vegas, and took his kitchen help, Miss Wren, with him to boot.

Walter purses his lips. "Don't trust 'em," he mutters.

"I won't." Senior's back straightens, standing at guard.

Miss Wren giggles, toddling up to the porch, a huge smile on her face. "It's Mrs. Brad Dingo White now. We got married in Vegas, but you can call me Pat."

Senior's brows press together, and he clasps his hands in front of him. "Congrats?"

Dingo plods toward the men, hand out to shake theirs. "How ya been? Man, it's good to see y'all."

"It is?"

"Hell, yeah. Put 'er there." He grabs Senior's hand, shakes it, then places his hands in prayer, gazing at Senior with sappy sorrowful eyes. "Listen. Man. I am so remorseful on how we parted company. I had a lot goin' on, you know? I wasn't right in the head, but the wife, she showed me the way."

Pat steps to her husband's side and hugs him.

"You gonna pay him back?" Walter nods to Senior.

"Oh." Pat's chin quivers. "We lost every dime in Vegas."

Dingo shrugs. "The virtual reality gaming thing didn't pan out. I guess I was before my time."

"Or a lazy dumbass who doesn't know shit about running a business."

"Please, we live in the truck," Pat says. "We had to beg for money at gas stations to get here, because I know in my heart, you'll forgive Bubby. Mr. Darling, you've been friends since Boy Scouts."

"Bubby?"

"Friends since Boy Scouts?" Senior grinds his teeth. He hates it when he does that, but he's doing his best to remain calm. "I just met him again last year since Boy Scouts, and apparently, I'm a bad judge of character."

Now Pat is gazing at him with tears in her big doe eyes, and that purple hair reminds him of a Manga character.

"Please? He needs a friend right now."

"We don't need friends of your sort." Walter thumbs. "Head on down the road."

"Oh, Bubby." Pat buries her face in Dingo's chest, sobbing.

Dingo hangs his head. "I don't blame you, man. We'll be on our way."

"I found her!" The distant shout belongs to Stitch. He trots toward the porch, pulling Mildred along.

"Slow down, damn it." She almost falls in her attempt to keep up.

Walter steps in front of them. "Where's the rest of yer crew?"

"I..." Mildred pants between words, "I'm the...only one."

Stitch's eyes are wide with excitement. "Found her inna cabin. She escaped from Caring Souls."

She plops onto a porch step. "That mile downhill..." Pants. "Seems more like ten."

"Hm, mm." Walter crosses his arms. "Thought you had me there...fer a minute."

Mildred stands to face Walter, inches away. "I didn't plan on getting stuck and yeah, you two," she points, "are clueless!"

Walter's mustache quivers. "Oh, yeah?"

"Yeah!"

"Okay, okay, break it up." Senior moves the two away from each other and takes Mildred gently by the shoulders. "Now, Mildred, why are you here by yourself?"

"She's evil. Her husband died, and now she's letting Caring Souls go to hell so she can ship us off." Tears float in the wells of her eyes.

"Mrs. Badmorn?"

"Yes, Mr. Darling, it's horrible there. Can't I just stay here?"

"But...Junior, isn't he...?"

"He's overwhelmed, trying his best, but Mrs. Badmorn is a steamroller."

Senior releases Mildred and pulls his cell phone from a back pocket. He taps on it. "I'm calling my son."

4

A MESS OF WHAT?

Junior faces his father, Dingo and Walter on the porch of the dining hall for the onslaught of questions. As soon as Mr. Badmorn passed away, Mrs. Badmorn let most of the staff go, refused cleaning service, and cut the budget in half. He's had to cover shifts with hardly three hours of sleep at night, his nerves are on edge, he must retrieve a runaway, and now explain to his dad why he's messing up.

"Well?" The expectant father asks.

"Mrs. Badmorn told me to tell you they aren't coming to Sedation Falls summer camp." Junior closes his eyes to keep spittle from his face when his dad shouts.

Walter claps his hands. "Hallelujah!"

Senior shouts, "What? Why the hell not?"

There it is, the letter T spit.

"She plans to shut down Caring Souls and turn it into a hotel spa. I'm calling families to take them out of there before she ships them all to God knows where."

"What about the state oversight?"

"You know how they are. They got like three people to oversee the whole state. They aren't gonna bother coming way up here. Besides, she got around all that because it's a private facility with less than thirty residents."

Dingo's mouth is hanging open. "Dang, you got a mess on yer hands."

"Remember Lana?"

Senior nods.

"She arrived this morning. I think something serious is going down."

Silas, the security guard and driver for Mrs. Badmorn, steps out of the black Cadillac Escalade he brought Junior in to retrieve Mildred. He stands wearing a dark suit and sunglasses, looming and intimidating; arms crossed.

Mildred grips Junior's arm. "Please. Please let me stay here."

Junior knows if Silas hears anything else he tells his father, things can go very badly for him. He takes Mildred's hand. "Good news. I talked to your sister. You're going to live with her."

Mildred's brows knit. "My sister? She lives in California."

"Right. You're catching a flight there tomorrow. We need to get back so you can pack."

"Well, if that isn't a whole new ball of wax. I haven't talked to my sister for three years since we got into a fight over politics."

Junior takes her arm and nervously glances toward Silas. "She's good now. Sisters gotta forget about those things, right? We need to get going."

"She has a bunch of deadbeat kids living with her. It's constant chaos." Mildred pulls away from Junior.

He leans in and whispers, "We really need to go now. Just humor me. Besides, things might be much better at your sister's."

"Fine. I'll come along...for you."

"Make sure you stay out of the toilet on the plane." Walter smirks.

"Oh you."

***

As Junior guides Mildred to the car, everyone else on the porch, Senior, Walter, Stitch, Dingo, and his new wife, Pat enter the dining hall and into the office.

Richard Darling Senior sits at his desk pushing the papers aside, and plants his face in his hands. Walter picks up the Jim Beam on his desk, takes a swig, and passes it to Miss Pat. She smells it, wrinkling her nose, and puts it back on the desk. Dingo picks it up and takes a big swallow of the brown liquid.

Walter leans on Senior's desk. "Looks like we got a problem, bud."

Dingo leans on the other side of the desk. "I'll say."

Senior lifts his face from his hands pulling the skin down—a sad hound dog. "Two weeks. We're only two weeks away and without Caring Souls, I don't even know who's coming. We're in debt to our eyeballs. Why did I ever do this?"

Dingo grins. "Cause you like adventure, Boy Scout."

"And old folks." Walter adds.

"Well, money would be nice too."

"Hey, that's where I come in." Dingo slaps Senior on the back.

"Huh?"

"I'm your ad man. Leave it to me. I'll get your campers."

"I can't pay you."

"I'll work on commission and wife here will do her kitchen job for free. How's that for ya? Just give us a place to sleep."

Miss Pat nods her head vigorously.

Walter, Stitch, and Senior go into a huddle, murmuring. After a few moments, Senior returns to his desk. "That's fine, but Miss Pat won't be in the kitchen. I promised that job to Leigh Ann. Miss Pat can oversee crafts."

Miss Pat's face implodes with disgust. "Crafts?"

Dingo wraps an arm around his wife's shoulder. "Come on, babe, beggars can't be choosers. It was your idea to come back here."

"Fine. But I'm doing it inside. There are too many bugs outside. You know I have a terrible fear of them, especially spiders. Ugh!" She shivers.

"Okay, we got a deal." Dingo thrusts a hand out and the men shake on it.

Stitch throws up his arms. "Happy ending." He heads to a closet to retrieve cleaning supplies. "Gotta go down an' clean the cabin Miss Mildred was in. Left a gedaufulous mess."

"A mess of what?" Walter asks.

Stitch raises a brow and shoots a *"you don't want to know look"*.

***

The TV in Senior's office is on. It used to be Junior's when he played video games. Senior likes background noise while he works.

"A summer camp built only for senior citizens in the foothills of the beautiful Blue Ridge Mountains."

A serene parklike setting is on the screen with the mountains in the background. There is a sailboat with a happy older couple snuggling in it on a lake. Then, another scene of them sitting beside each other on lounge chairs by a swimming pool. Senior turns up the volume. It looks like competition. Another camp got the same idea?

"Activities abound, with fun for every level of physical activity."

Old people are playing pickle ball. Others are bicycling on a lovely tree lined path.

"No wonder I've only had a few sign-ups. Wow looks nice."

"And only the best farm raised locally sourced meals prepared by a James Beard awarded chef."

People are sitting at cloth covered tables being served by uniformed waiters.

"All topped by fantastic evening entertainment."

A group of seniors are surrounding a craps table and cheering. Another segment shows a guy singing and playing guitar.

"Damn, I even want to go there."

"All this and more at..." The camera pans out to an aerial shot of something that looks familiar...the dining hall. *"Camp Sedation Falls. At Camp Sedation Falls, find*

out what being truly sedate means. Call now. Camp Seda-tion Falls...send your folks there."

"Dingo!" Senior's phone lights up.

5

OPENING DAY

Cars line up along the lane to Camp Sedation Falls as Stitch flags one at a time into a parking spot. The ten slots in front of the dining hall had filled up in minutes, forcing him to run out and direct folks to the field near the softball diamond.

Stitch waves a yellow flag erratically in his attempts to direct traffic. "Oh Lawd, this is madness."

BEEP! BEEP! "Tyrone!"

Stitch's stringy arms and legs fly at the shock, dropping his flag.

"You hoo! It's me, Bethany."

He scoops up the flag, darting away from the car just before impact.

"Oopsy, Tiffy, you nearly hit the poor thing. Stop the car."

The silver sedan skids to a stop in the gravel. Stitch brushes dirt from his shirt and forces himself to smile despite his desire to run up to the driver and choke the shit out of her. He swivels around to face Bethany gawking at him from the passenger's window. Her wide-set googly eyes could belong to an ostrich. "Are you alright, honey?"

Stitch sucks in a breath to bring back his loopy self. "H...hello, Miss Bethany."

"We were looking for a parking spot and didn't see you there." Bethany cups one side of her mouth and whispers, "She's a bad driver."

A voice over her shoulder shouts, "I heard that."

"Welcome back." Stitch points with his flag. "There's a spot over yonder."

Bethany turns toward the voice. "You see where you're supposed to go?"

"I see it. I ain't blind."

Bethany cups a hand beside her mouth again. "Remember my bully story?" She thumbs behind her. "That was Tiffy, but we're friends now...aren't we?"

Tiffany guns the auto, throwing gravel. Stitch shakes his head. "Lawd, Lawd, Lawd."

A motorcycle rumbles up beside him. It's a Honda Goldwing with crash bars in the front. Stitch marvels at how anyone can hold up a bike like that. The passenger seat resembles an easy chair with speakers for arm rests, and there are saddle bags on the sides and a trunk on the back. The front of the motorcycle has a big faring and windshield. *No wonder it has roll bars...my Lawd.*

The guy riding it looks about as skinny as he is with long grey hair tied in a ponytail. The woman on the back is much sturdier, with long pitch-black hair tied down with a bandana. The guy removes sunglasses two times bigger than his face. "Whew, man. I'm glad I stayed far behind that car. She almost wiped out somebody turning in. People over ninety shouldn't have driver's licenses...know what I mean?"

The woman behind him playfully slaps him in the arm. "She wasn't ninety...eighty maybe."

Stitch grins wide. "Welcome to Sedation Falls."

The biker shakes his hand. "I'm Harley, and the sweet thang on the back is Kelly. We saw the TV commercial an' thought, why not? Second honeymoon. Besides, it's a great area fer ridin'."

The woman on the back hugs him from behind. "You got that, Babe."

Stitch gasps, *The ad!* He wipes the sweat from his forehead with the flag. "I'm Tyrone. They call me Stitch. I sure hope we'll meet your expectations. You can park your bike at your cabin."

"See there?" Harley revs the motorcycle. "Already front row seats. Thanks, little buddy." He lets out the clutch and eases the bike onto the field.

There goes Harley on his Honda. Strange world.

Once everyone is parked, Stitch runs to the dining hall where the staff awaits new arrivals. Nurse Oyomama is collecting medicines, Senior is checking in campers and visiting families. Counselor Leigh Ann is standing there appearing miserable as usual, rolling her eyes while pushing her glasses back onto the bridge of her nose. Samantha, Walter's granddaughter, is going to be the new lifeguard. She finished college but failed her first bar exam. Chef Fry seems to have lost fifty pounds and looks mean and lean. Chef just finished cooking school at Asheville Mountain Kitchen. He's pretty sure nobody there was called James Beard. Anyways, it'll be great to eat real food instead of the peanut butter sand-wiches and pot pies Stitch has been living on for the past months. Being the camp manager got him a nice permanent cabin, but not a chef, and a cook he ain't.

"Git the gas on!"

The shock sends an electrical current down Stitch's spine. "Eek!"

It's Walter. "What ya standin' around day-dreamin' for? Git yer ass over there."

"Yes, sir. But, what about..."

Walter holds up a knapsack, "I'm settin' up the scav-enger hunt."

"Oh? And how about..."

"No hula dancers this year. Bob got us a Scottish Highland group."

"Coolio."

"Yeah, since yer turned on by men in skirts."

Stitch crosses his arms squeezing his eyes shut. "Well, not that way...I mean..."

Without another word, Walter saunters toward the woods, swinging the knapsack to his back. Stitch knows it's not for hiding anything for a scavenger hunt. Walter is on his way to smoke pot in his new lounge in the woods he calls a chapel.

Several campers from last year have returned. Kim, who was born in Korea, is checking in with her two adult children, Jane and Joe. She's wearing her floppy fishing hat as always. Stitch approaches her. "Hi, Miss Kim, so good to see you ba..."

"When do we feesh?"

"Fish? Well, Mr. Evans and Mr. Darlin' put some peddle boats on the lake. They think it'll be more relaxin' and 'sides, I think you got all the fish last year."

"Bah!" Kim waves his comment away. "Feeshing is relaxing."

Stitch raises a brow. "Not the way you do it. It's madness stickin' your arm in a hole dangling it for a catfish. A snappin' turtle could snatch it right off."

Kim steps up to him. Even though he's short, she's shorter. She tilts her face up to Stitch's, eyes glaring. "What you know 'bout noodlin'?"

Jane takes her by the arm. "Come on, Mami. You'll still have fun, fishing or not."

"I still feesh," Kim declares as Jane guides her away.

Stitch places a hand on his hip wagging his head back and forth. "I ain't gonna stop her. She'll do what she wants anyways."

He lopes toward the campers Richard Darling Senior is checking in. Scottish Bob, Walter's old roommate, has returned. Max, Bethany, and Muffy are there as well. Stitch spies Muffy's family who came for the day, but there is no sign of Doug. Muffy's three grandchildren run off to swim, while Samantha chases from behind.

"Hello, Miss Muffy." Stitch believes she is the kindest lady on the planet.

Muffy gives him a warm hug. "Tyrone! Oh, I've missed you so much, especially since..." She tears up and her daughter, Melody, rushes to her side.

"It's okay, honey." Muffy pats Melody's arm. "My Dougie passed on six months ago." Melody hands her a Kleenex and she dabs her eyes. "A newlywed widow."

Muffy takes the handle of her suitcase and rolls it down the walkway toward her cabin.

Another one of her daughters, Menda, elbows Stitch and winks. "Believe me. He died a happy man." She hollers beside his ear while pointing toward the pool. "Ronnie, git yer trunks on! Naked swimmin' is not allowed here!"

With ears ringing, Stitch asks Richard Darling Senior if Charles and Minerva are coming. In between shaking campers' hands and introductions, he answers, "Not this year. Their daughter just had a baby. New grandparents, ya know?"

Stitch shakes his head, *no.*

"Anyway," Senior smiles. The smile appears to Stitch to be more like a constipated grimace. "You see Walter...Mr. Evans around?"

"Yeah." Stitch points toward the woods. "He's at Chapel. Said he's hidin' stuff for the scavenger hunt."

Senior rolls his eyes. "Uh huh, right."

Bagpipes break the tension. Four men in Scottish Tartan kilts swagger onto the grass beside the dining hall. Two are playing bagpipes, while the other two, including Scottish Bob, beat on drums. Campers and families gather and applaud.

Dingo jumps up on a picnic table and shouts, "Welcome campers and families. Boy, do we have a show for you. I hope you all had time to check out your cabins. Returning campers, did you notice each one now has its own bathroom?"

Bob's mouth hangs open in awe. "Praise be."

"And after lunch, when your families go home, we'll give you a tour of our fantastic facilities and end it with fun!"

Applause.

Everyone enters the dining hall for the program. Chef Fry and Leigh Ann hustle into the kitchen to prepare lunch. Samantha herds wet children inside to sit with Muffy's family.

***

The bagpipes and drumming resume. Melody taps her mother's arm. "Scottish Bob looks pretty good in a kilt, doesn't he?"

Muffy blushes and tosses her shoulder length blonde hair; a color she has maintained since her cheerleader days. Just because Dougie has passed on, it doesn't mean she should let herself go. She may be seventy-five but looks more like fifty-five thanks to Oil of Old Age, hair coloring, Botox, Liposuction, and good make-up. She bats her false eyelashes. "Yes, he does, and I love his brogue accent."

Menda waves at the round table where her family is sitting. "Where's the white table cloths?"

"What do you mean?" Muffy snaps out of her day-dream.

"The ad said we would be sitting at tables covered with white table cloths and we would be served by fancy waiters."

"Here?"

Menda sits and slaps her palms onto the table. "Yeah."

Her three children, Leroy, Ronnie, and Maya mimic her, and slap their hands on the table. "Yeah!"

She glances around. "Where's the waiter?"

Muffy places her hand on top of Menda's. "I have no idea what you are talking about. We've never had anything like that."

"Then, you've been ripped off. It was right there on TV."

A man sitting at a table nearby shouts, "On Facebook too."

Menda stands and yells, "Waiter!"

Leigh Ann steps out from the kitchen and smiles the best Leigh Ann can smile, which appears to be more of a scowl. "Lunch is ready. Please line up and we will serve you at the counter."

The man bellows, "No waiter?"

Leigh Ann nods. "No, sir."

As guests and campers line up for their meal, the man glares with anger. "That's it! C'mon, Ethel, we've been gypped."

"Herbert, what do you expect for two-hundred dollars a day?" She throws up her arms. "All inclusive."

Herbert marches out of the dining hall. Ethel turns to the guests watching the whole thing. "I'm sorry, he's a cheapskate." She walks out behind him.

Muffy wonders if others will follow them. She loves Sedation Falls and white table cloths and waiters have no business at a camp for God's sake. Her family hesitantly gets in line behind her.

Menda sniffs and leans to get a better look at what is being served. "Is that chicken pot pie?"

Muffy smiles, proud of this camp. "Yes, and home-made. Chef may not be a James Beard winner, but he's a hell of a cook."

***

Walter strolls into his clearing in the woods which now have two rows of wooden benches facing a pulpit. He calls it a chapel, but it's really a comfortable place to smoke his pot. On either side of the pulpit are rocking chairs with small side tables made from stumps. He sits on one of the rockers, knapsack on his lap. He reaches into his bag, pulls out a baggy of weed and rolling papers, and prepares his joint. "I don't mind puttin' my two cents into the camp, but I sure as hell ain't gonna kowtow to the campers neither. All I need is a toilet in my cabin an' this here chapel." He lights up his smoke, takes a long drag, and holds his breath. "Good shit," he wheezes, before allowing the THC inhabited smoke to exit his lungs.

Snapping twigs nearby. Walter sits up at attention. He cocks his head and listens. Something sounding like a mix between a baby and a sheep calls, "Ma!"

"Who's there?"

From the edge of the clearing a bear cub waddles toward him, then another. "Shit, what's in this pot?" Walter's mustache quivers while the cubs approach him sniffing his legs. He lifts them away as high as he can, which isn't very far. One cub paws at his foot. "Shoo! Shoo!"

Their mother can't be far. I could get mauled to death. His stomach aches from holding his legs up, and the cub is gnawing his shoe. The second one calls out, *Ma,* and runs to the edge of the clearing. Walter shuts his eyes and holds his breath while his life flashes before him. *Shit, shit, shit.*

Something big is shuffling through the leaves heading straight for him. It stops only a few feet away. Walter's heart skips. He'll be meeting his dearly departed wife soon. The cubs have quit batting and gnawing on him. He places his feet down and waits for the end.

Nothing. The bear is still near. He smells its earthy musk. He can hear it panting. The shuffling of leaf litter tells him the cubs are playing. Walter slowly opens his eyes and lifts his head.

"Rizzy!" Relief washes over him at the recognition of his bear buddy. Why, the animal let Walter pick ticks off its head. Only a true buddy would do that. He glances at the cubs, then Rizzy, when a realization comes to him. "These yours?"

Rizzy is sitting and nodding her head up and down. The smallest cub snuggles under her to suckle. The other follows suit.

"Well, I'll be damned. You're a gal!"

She lies down to finish nursing and nudges her cubs.

"Nice family you got there." Walter glances about. "Hope the father ain't nearby."

Rizzy closes her eyes in contentment. Walter does too.

***

"There you are you old coot!"

Walter jerks awake to ostrich-eyed Bethany pecking at him. "Shit, not you." Groggy, he searches for Rizzy. "Where..."

"Yeah, it's me, and I can't find any of your scavenger hunt items. It's a rip off."

Tiffany peeks over Bethany's shoulder. "Who's this guy?"

The woman looking over Bethany's shoulder has bushy eyebrows. Walter never saw a woman with such bushy eyebrows. They make her look like she's constantly pissed off about something. Maybe she is.

"I hid them, you just ain't no good at findin' them."

"Oh yeah?" Bethany's hands on her hips pecking away. "I know you, Walter Evans."

He stands and stretches. "Listen." Walter picks up his bag. "Keep an eye out fer bears. Rizzy has cubs."

Ostrich eyes stumbles backwards, glancing about frantically. "What?"

***

Knowing there's a slim chance Walter hid stuff for the scavenger hunt, Stitch takes items on the campers lists and hides them. He must hide a few in the woods. He hates the woods. Too many wild animals that could eat him are in there. Just as Stitch is bending down to hide a red solo cup, it happens. He stands unmoving—except for knees knocking together. His eyes are squinched tightly closed while holding his breath. Two bear cubs sniff his feet. One swats at his shaking knees.

6

BEARS AND BEDLAM

As the Scottish band is performing their finale Harley shouts, "Play some Skynyrd, man."

Bethany shoots an indignant glare. Kelly elbows him.

"What?" I was jus' funnin' with them." The next number sounds remarkably familiar. "What the..." Harley's jaw is agape. The band is performing "Free Bird" on bagpipes and drums.

They finish to a standing ovation with Harley leading the call.

***

Meanwhile, Stitch is praying with everything in his soul to survive the oncoming attack. He will be eaten alive, leftovers served to the cubs.

"Listen, I ain't good to eat. Look at me, I'm all skin and bone. Whatever meat y'all git'll prolly be greasy." Stitch slowly raises his right hand. "I swear."

Mama bear shambles through the brush.

"Please God, I ain't old enough to go yet...not this way, anyhow."

Mama bear grunts low. Stitch faints. The bears trot to their Mama. The three of them return to the shelter of the woods.

Stitch awakens to Walter staring down at him. He jumps up and hugs the human.

"What the hell you doin'?" Walter pushes Stitch off him.

"Bears! There were bears all over me. I...I was goin' to be their dinner."

"Shit, son, that was Rizzy and her cubs. She was showin' 'em off to ya," Walter chuckles.

"Oh, no." Stitch grabs his head with both hands. "It's a girl. We're gonna be swarmin' wif bears. How am I gonna live?" He feels faint again.

"They don't want yer skinny ass, believe me." Walter waves while moving out of the woods.

Stitch stands, eyes glistening near tears. "I...I'll believe you." He runs to catch up.

As Stitch and Walter approach the dining hall, the band is packing up. Bethany and Tiffany are huffing and puffing, faces contorted into frustration. Richard Darling Senior is paying the musicians when the girls accost him. Stitch rushes to Senior's aid.

Bethany holds out a banged and bent red solo cup and a yellow wiffle ball. "Look at this!" She shoves the items under Senior's nose. "This is all we could find in Walter's stupid scavenger hunt."

Tiffany shoves a crumpled piece of paper into his chest. "And there are like fifteen things on here! This is a scam."

Senior raises both arms in surrender. "Ladies, ladies, please..."

Stitch arrives on the scene huffing and puffing to catch his breath. "There you are." He gasps. "You two are the big winners of the hunt."

"What?" Bethany holds her items under Stitch's nose. "We only found two things."

Stitch places his hands on his hips, still panting to breathe. "Well, we ran into a little glitch. The bears ate some of the stuff an'...."

"I found one!" Kim runs toward the group. "A rock."

Tiffany checks her paper. "Oh yeah, one of the items IS a rock."

Bethany snatches the paper and studies it. "A painted rock. We never found a painted rock."

"I did." Kim holds her rock high in the air. It fits in her hand with blobs of blue, yellow, and orange covering the surface of the stone. She shows it to the group.

"What's it supposed to be?" Tiffany asks.

Stitch feels a bead of sweat track along a cheek. "Um, Walter painted it, so he did hide the stuff."

"See, I told ya." Walter joins the group discussion. "I might be a fibber, but I ain't no liar."

Bethany squints an ostrich eye at him. "Why you..."

"Listen, listen!" Senior waves his arms as though breaking up a fight. "Everyone that found something on the list is winners. How's that?"

"What we git?" Kim drops her rock.

"Uh...um..." Senior stammers.

"Miss Kim, you get to fish all day tomorrow." Stitch stands proud.

She jumps up and down with glee. "I brought new pole."

"And Miss Bethany and Miss Tiffany, you just won yourselves a pool boy. I'll be at your beck and call for a day." Senior bows.

Tiffany's brows arch high on her forehead. "You'll even serve us drinks?"

Senior nods. It's more of a sideways stretch.

"With alcohol?" Bethany leans toward him.

"Yes."

"Wee!"

Tiffany laughs, "This place doesn't suck so bad after all."

"Let's check out our cabin." Bethany takes Tiffany by the arm, and they stroll down the path.

Walter slaps Senior on the back. "You made yer bed, now you gotta mess it up agin."

"Don't you mean, lie in it?"

"You ain't gonna have time fer lyin," Walter chuckles, his eyebrows bounce as if they're laughing too.

***

"What the hell did we sign up for? This ain't nothin' like the commercial." Harley paces the cabin while Kelly unpacks.

"I like it, it's rustic—with a nice new bathroom."

"It don't look like the one on TV. It had marble floors. We were conned."

Kelly steps in front of Harley. "Cool your jets. That commercial was so bougie. That isn't us, this is. I'm glad it's not like the commercial. I mean, you seriously wanted all that hoopty-do shit?"

Harley's bottom lip curls out. "A spa woulda been nice."

"Listen, I'll give you a nice massage later if you settle your ass down, okay?" Kelly rubs his shoulders.

Harley closes his eyes and sighs. "I thought we were gettin' a deal—cheap luxury, you know?"

"Babe, there is luxury in simplicity."

"Simplicity? Did you see that big ass Tiki god by the pool? I swear it looks like that Walter guy."

"Mr. Evans?"

"Yeah. It seems to stare through me—gives me the creeps...an' talk about old, everyone here 'cept for the counselors are at least a dozen years older than us."

"Well, it did say it's an over fifty camp."

"I'd say way over fifty."

Kelly plops onto the bed and strokes the quilt spread. "I like it here. Let's make the best of it, okay?"

Harley sits next to her. The mattress is firm, but not too firm. He wraps an arm around her and shrugs, "What the hell?" He kisses her, pulling her down with him onto the bed.

***

Walter walks into his cabin to the face of Scottish Bob, "Shit, I gotta room with you agin?"

Bob is unpacking his bag. "Twas the last bed left."

"You better not have a coffee can in there." Walter stands in the bathroom door pointing at the facilities. "We got a bathroom now...with a toilet!"

"Praise be, dee best news eva'." Bob pats his stomach. "I nay need it afta' those braw meat pies. I hadn't a pie that well tidy scran' since I was a wee lad." He begins to remove his kilt.

Walter covers his eyes with his hands. "God...uh, do ya gotta do that now? Can't ya wait till I'm outta here? Dag nab it."

Bob chuckles. "I dinna wear what nature blessed me unda' me kilt. I have knickers on, see?"

Walter peeks between his fingers. Bob is standing before him in khaki shorts while holding his skirt aloft. "Whew, had me goin' there fer a minute."

"I'm mighty proud of yer efforts ta keepin' yer swearin' in check."

"It ain't easy, let me tell you." Walter bows deeply. "But I aim to please."

***

Tiffany and Bethany are in their cabin unpacking.

Tiffany pulls the sheets down on one of the two full-size beds. "This bed is mine." She picks up the pillow, fluffing it. "Hm, seems a bit flat. I'm a side sleeper. You got an extra one?"

Bethany shakes her head *no*, while pulling her sheets down. She draws a pillow from her suitcase and places it on top of the one on the bed.

"Wait a minute." Tiffany yanks the pillow out from under the one Bethany brought. "Yes, you do."

"But I sleep with two pillows." Bethany steps up to Tiffany who is a foot taller than her and all muscle. *Maybe asking nicely will work.* She holds out a hand. "Please give it back?"

Tiffany waves her off, turning to finish unpacking. "Get one at the front desk."

"Front desk? This isn't a hotel."

"Whatever, I'm sure they have a spare somewhere."

There it is. Just like the old days when Tiffany always gets her way. She used to call Bethany *Ostrich*, and Bethany called Tiffany *Toofis*, for her large teeth, but she grew into them, and now Toofis is a statuesque six foot two.

Tiffany steps into the bathroom with a bottle of facial cream, spreading it by the spoonful onto her face. "So, what's on the agenda for tomorrow? I hope it's not as lame as that scavenger hunt."

"That scavenger hunt sucked because ol' Walter was in charge of it. At least he helped save the camp. I gotta give him that." Bethany enters the bathroom to talk to Tiffany, who now has pads covering her eyes, and whitening strips glued to her teeth. It's a hideous sight.

"Bt, er brr a gmma fer wrk ow," Tiffany mumbles through the strips.

"A gym? You need a gym? This is a camp. You get your workout with group actlvitics."

"Fu...? Br brr be fn."

"You'll have fun if you keep an open mind about it, sheesh." Bethany plops onto her one-pillow bed and waits for Tiffany to finish her beauty ritual...which isn't working.

***

Muffy and Kim are sitting on the porch of the cabin they are sharing. Muffy closes her eyes and breathes in the fresh evening air. "They really fixed this place up. I'm glad Walter is helping the boys out. I knew he wasn't all bad."

Kim glances about but doesn't answer.

"Wasn't Bobby cute in his kilt? I didn't know he could play the drums."

Kim smirks. "I can play da drums. Easy."

"I'm sure you can, but you need to have rhythm."

Kim grabs the arms of her rocking chair and glares at Muffy. "I have rhythm." She squats to the floor and pounds on the planks. "See?"

Muffy holds her ears, squinching her eyes shut. "Okay, okay, you have rhythm. Please stop, you'll wake the dead."

Kim stands. "Let's noodle."

Shocked, Muffy's eyes grow large until a moment later, she remembers what Kim is talking about. "You mean, fish, don't you?"

Kim nods.

"Like, stick my arm in a hole underwater until a catfish snatches it?"

"Uh, huh. Now. Night feeshing is da best."

Muffy grimaces. "Um...gee. I would, but I'm wiped out. You go ahead, you little Korean firecracker. Where do you get all your energy?"

Kim doesn't answer. She struts into the cabin. After a few minutes, comes out bedecked in her khaki fishing hat and rubber gloves that go up to her elbows. She bows to Muffy before going on her way.

"Be safe," Muffy calls out to her.

"What a pussy," Kim mumbles.

Muffy jumps to her feet. "I heard that. I am not. I just don't want to lose an arm to whatever is lurking in that lake."

"Whatever."

***

BAM BAM BAM. Pounding on Max's door. He leaps out of bed in boxer shorts and answers it. He's supposed to have a cabin mate, but he canceled at the last minute. *Must be the new guy.*

Max opens the door and faces Kim. His hand instinctively covers his privates in case he has morning wood, even though it's midnight. "This is a surprise. Are you okay? Need help?"

"I need side man."

"At this hour?"

"Night feeshing is da best."

"Okay, give me a minute to get dressed."

Kim sits cross-legged on the porch and waits.

Once dressed, Max walks with Kim to the Camp's Lake Watchawanna. The full moon makes it easy to see the dock. There is a row of four peddle boats parked beside it.

Max taps Kim on the shoulder. "Look at that. They have boats on the lake now."

Her face shows no interest. "Uh, huh, we feesh."

"Okay, but maybe we can try one when we're done?"

She shrugs. "Maybe." Kim wades into the murky water and suddenly sucks in a gasp of air from the chill.

"It's been a cooler than average spring," Max calls from shore. "You, okay?"

Kim shivers. "I'm fine." She leans forward into the dark lake, her arm moving back and forth, searching.

Max is relieved his job is to grab the fish when she tosses it onto the shore. The lake reminds him of one he saw in a slasher movie not long ago. Creepy. She wades around, feeling for several minutes. He wants to go back to bed. "Anything?"

"No ting. It's too cold, feesh hide, not want to bite."

"Come on out. It's getting late, and I don't want you to get Hypothermia."

Kim wades out of the lake to Max's relief. She's soaked to the bone. He wraps his arms around her to get her warm. She snuggles into his chest.

Max hasn't hugged a woman in a long time. It warms him even though both of them are soggy. "Um...I forgot a towel."

She burrows. "Not a problem."

"Let's get into one of those boats. It'll be warmer, and we can sit."

They step into one of the peddle boats. Max wraps his arm around her and Kim leans into him. He has always liked Kim—she makes him laugh, but right now, it seems to be something more. He wants to kiss her. "This is nice, isn't it?" Maybe chatter will get his mind off it.

Kim faces him, her gaze seeming to lock onto his heart. Max is certain she can hear it thumping. He leans forward and their lips touch—soft and lingering.

"Okay, side man. We go back now."

Kim has broken the spell.

***

"This feels so weird. I should be with my husband." Miss Pat, who is now Mrs. Dingo, is laying out a sleeping bag on the floor of Leigh Ann and Samantha's cabin.

"Thanks to your husband's ad, we are full. There isn't another cabin for you guys." Leigh Ann sniffs.

"You're right, and believe me, this is better than sleeping in that truck." Miss Pat wiggles into her bag.

Samantha sits on the edge of her bed. "You were really living in your truck?"

"Yes, it was rough, but it takes a big man to admit his mistakes, and he made some big ones, but I love him no matter what. Dingo never intended to steal from the camp. I mean, he did give Senior the down payment. Vegas was horrible. We lost everything within a few months. I begged him to come here in hopes Mr. Darling would take us back. I'm grateful he gave us another chance. Hopefully, everything is even Steven now." Miss Pat adjusts her pillow.

Samantha stands. "Wow, listen, take my bed, I can sleep on the floor."

Miss Pat waves her off. "Oh, no, honey. You don't need too...well, okay." She gets out of the bag and carries it to the bed.

Samantha takes a pillow and blanket and settles on the floor.

"You're sweet. I would've stayed on the floor, but I totally hate spiders. I would die if one crawled on my face while I was sleeping." Miss Pat cuddles into her sleeping bag on the bed. "Goodnight."

Leigh Ann chuffs, "Good luck. Glad I'm not as nice as you, Sam. Goodnight."

"Shit," Samantha mumbles, glancing about for bugs.
***

"Hey man, thanks for lettin' me bunk up with y'all." Dingo is pulling out a futon in Stitch's cabin while Stitch and Chef Fry settle into bunks.

Chef rolls over on the bottom bunk. "We didn't have a choice."

"Now, come on, let's let by-gones be by-gones. If it makes ya happy, karma bit me in the ass." Dingo approaches Chef to shake his hand.

Chef Fry climbs out of his bunk and stretches. "Jus' make sure you never order the groceries from here on out. I'll take care of that. I got a degree now."

"Degree?"

Stitch rolls off the top bunk, landing on his feet. "Yeah, man, big Chef Fry here got a scholarship from Asheville Mountain Kitchen. He pats the chef on the back, a wide smile planted on his face.

Chef stands stoic, serious. "So, stay out of the kitchen, and we good."

"Yeah, yeah, no problem. I promise." Dingo and Chef shake hands.

Stitch approaches Dingo, chin jutting forward. "An' long as you in my home, you best be respectful."

Dingo raises his brows and claps his hands. "Oh, now I get it. I thought all the cabins looked like this." He strolls to a corner containing a small refrigerator, microwave, and coffee pot. "I thought, wow, not only do all the cabins have shitters, but they got all the trappin's of a four-star hotel. Dang, a coffee pot and everythin'."

Stitch blushes through the brown of his skin. "I wouldn't go that far. I'm the property manager now. I take care of the place off season, so I live here. You're sleepin' on MY furniture."

Dingo's hands rest on his hips while gazing about. "Wow isn't that generous of Senior. Maybe you can use a co-manager?"

"He don't need no help," Chef Fry's voice booms.

Dingo raises his arms in defense. "Okay, okay, just floating out an idea is all. Once the wife an' I get back on our feet, we'll move on. I get it." Dingo lies on the futon and fluffs the sofa pillow.

Stitch climbs the ladder back to the top bunk, while Chef works his six-foot, two-hundred-and-forty-pound frame into the bottom bunk. "Damn, glad I lost weight." His feet stick out through the rungs of the ladder. "An' Mr. White!"

"Yeah?"

"No snorin' neither."

"Um, I'll try."

***

Senior pulls the woolen blanket from the cot in his office. The mattress is covered in seeds and crumbs of some kind. He brushes them off and studies a few morsels concerned they could be mouse droppings. He reaches into a garbage bag he brought from home and pulls out a clean set of sheets and a comforter. He searches for a pillow. "Shit, I forgot one." Senior balls up a jacket. "That'll have to do." He gets into bed wearing shorts and a T-shirt.

The things Junior was saying are keeping him from sleep. Mr. Badmorn has died and now, Mrs. Badmorn is going to close Caring Souls and turn it into a spa. And Lana is there. Why? She's a purchaser. What is Mrs. Badmorn purchasing? Not this camp. As stressful as it is, people here need this place—not some over-priced spa hotel. *She can shove it up her ass. Lana too.*

7

FOR NOW

The rumbling of heavy machinery, jack hammers, and beeps of trucks backing up rouses Senior from sleep. He jumps out of his cot and runs to the window. The machinery is operating right beside the dining hall and on the hill toward Caring Souls Adult Center. Men are using chainsaws to clear trees, creating a mile long path. A huge roller in front of another truck is flattening the road. Hot asphalt permeates the air so thick he can taste it.

Senior grabs a pair of shorts, pulling on them while rushing outside. The gravel hurts his bare feet, so he runs back inside and throws on a pair of flip-flops. Several other campers are gazing about the grounds, yawning, scratching their heads, and holding their noses. Senior storms to the closest man wearing a yellow safety vest and grimy white hard hat.

"What the hell is going on?" he shouts over the din.

"What does it look like? We're building a road," the man shouts back.

"But this is my camp." Senior wants to appear menacing, but it's a chilly morning. He crosses his arms in front of his chest.

The man shrugs. "Talk to the supervisor."

Walter marches up to Senior, mustache twitching like a squirrel on an electric fence. "What the fuck is goin' on?"

"They're paving a road."

"To where?"

"I think to Caring Souls. I need to find a man in charge. They're on our property."

A black Limo motors up the lane from the main road and parks in front of the dining hall. The driver, Silas, steps out and opens the back passenger door. A woman carrying a huge leopard bag takes his hand. Even in sunglasses, her hair in a tight bun, Senior knows who she is. His heart flutters but he pushes the feeling away reminding himself that her affection toward him was only a way to get what she wanted. When she didn't get it, he was stepped on like a cockroach, and drilled into the dirt by her four-inch heel. He steels himself and approaches her.

"Lana, I should have known you have something to do with this?" Senior scowls, waves toward the new road.

She tilts her head, putting weight on one leg and holds up her cell phone. "The foreman called me."

"Why you? You're a purchasing agent." Realization slaps him in the face. "Wait a minute...you're the supervisor too?"

She glares at him like someone would at a puppy who tore up the couch. Walter nudges him aside to face Lana. Silas moves to stop him, but Lana waves him away.

Walter spits. "You git yer monkeys off our property."

Silas reaches into the car. The men freeze in place. He brings out a "No Trespassing" sign and strolls to the edge of the woods where Walter's chapel is located.

"Son of a biscuit eater. What the hell is he doin?"

Lana hands him a piece of paper. He passes it on to Senior and both men study the illustration. It is a survey of purchased property. The only area not outlined is the camp itself. Everything else, including the property between Sedation Falls and Caring Souls is marked as sold.

The butterflies in Senior's gut, mixed with the angry buzz of bees in his mind cause his whole body to shake. His hands ball into fists. "I bought this property!"

Lana smirks. "Apparently you didn't study the plat. You and your pal were only interested in outbidding me. I'm amazed your camp has lasted this long."

"Pal?" Walter asks.

Senior turns to him and shakes his head, the corners of his mouth turned down. "Dingo."

"This is fucked up." Walter's bushy brows are butting heads.

Lana smiles. Her derisive grin reminds Senior of a villain in a Disney movie. "You still have your little camp." She begins to enter the limo, stops and leans out with one high-heeled foot still on the ground. "For now."

Campers are surrounding Walter and Senior grousing about what is going on as the car moves up the lane toward Caring Souls. Senior raises his arms. "Everything is fine. There's a delicious breakfast waiting for you all and afterward, meet back here for field events. We'll just have to deal with a bit of noise."

"And smell," Kim shouts.

Harley joins in. "This ain't what I paid for!"

Senior swallows the lump forming in his throat. A vision of his retirement is a dollar bill on wings flitting away. "Nobody is forcing you to be here. I'll personally give you your deposit back." He feels in his pocket for his lucky penknife. He was lucky when he found it on this very property and his son, Junior, shined it up. The luck hasn't kicked in this time yet, but he rubs it anyway.

Kelly turns her face up to Harley shaking her head. He hugs her and waves. "Naw, it's okay, dawg. I've stayed in worse places."

The crowd breaks up as campers relax and chat among themselves while strolling to breakfast in the dining hall. Senior is relieved Chef Fry is an even better cook this year.

"Dodged another bullet there, partner, but what are we gonna do bout my woods?" Walter's bristly bearded jaw juts toward them.

"You may be forced out." Senior avoids eye contact with Walter and studies the ground. He vigorously rubs on his knife. "How did I miss the acres we didn't own? I know I signed for forty-five." He rubs his head.

"It is 'bout forty-five acres, dumbass. The camp is it."

"I thought it was more."

"Holy shit, I bet you flunked geometry."

Senior's face burns with embarrassment. "Almost."

"Well, that explains it. Look." Walter waves toward the dining hall. "An acre adds up to forty-three thousand, five-hundred and sixty square feet. Sounds like a lot, but a square mile is six-hundred and forty acres. We got less than ten percent of that. Boy, look up when I'm talkin' to ya."

Senior forces himself to look Walter in the eyes. They are the eyes of a man with tenderness deep inside, no matter how hard he tries to hide it under those wiry brows.

Walter continues, "So, we got the mess hall, parking lot, cabins, lake, and pool. We ain't got most of the woods, the ball field, and that damn road up the hill to Caring Souls. An' I would swear to my dead wife's grave, the chapel is mine."

Senior's stomach is so knotted up, he wants to throw up. "This is why I lost my job at PS Energy. I miss details. We are screwed."

Walter places a hand on Senior's shoulder. "We'll find a way. My daughter may have failed her first bar exam, but she's smart. If Badmorn finds a loophole, we'll find a bigger one. Guaranteed."

The tightness in Senior's shoulders relax. He releases the death grip on the penknife in his pocket. "Thanks, Walter."

"I jus' want her to stay the hell outta my chapel."

"You care about this camp. Admit it."

Walter cracks his neck while walking away and mumbles, "Dip shit."

***

While Silas drives, Lana is texting Mrs. Badmorn when she spies something brown from the corner of her eye. It's a bear and cubs approaching the road into the path of the limo.

Lana leans forward, eyes wild and screaming, "Stop, stop, stop!"

"Shit!"

8

THE CHASE

The car swerves like a shark through a school of menhaden. Silas slams on the brakes. The limo jumps a ditch and lurches straight for a tree. Lana covers her head, bracing for impact. The front passenger side slams against the trunk of the oak. Silence. Lana sits up and runs her hands over her face and arms checking for any injuries.

Silas rubs the side of his head. "I wrenched my neck. Are you hurt?"

Lana massages a sore thigh. "No. No, I think I'm okay."

Silas pushes the deflated airbag away from him. He dabs a finger to his bloody nose. "Fuckin' airbags."

"Maybe we should call an ambulance. Neck injuries are nothing to mess with."

"No!" Silas stiffly turns toward Lana. "I'm fine. Just sore is all." He tilts up his head, squeezing his nostrils together. "You got a Kleenex?"

A distant sound like a sheep's cry. "Ma! Ma!"

Lana closes her eyes tight. "Oh my God, we hit its mother."

"GROWL!"

Lana's eyes snap open. Rizzy's muzzle is against her window. Silas pushes at his door.

"No! Stop! She'll attack you."

Rizzy rambles to Silas's window, growling and pawing. Silas fumbles for the glove box and pulls out a gun.

"Ma!" A cub's cry.

"Don't shoot her! She has babies. Oh God, I hope you didn't run over one."

Lana and Silas search through the windshield. They don't see anything.

Silas leans away from the driver's side window pointing his gun. "If she breaks that window, I'm shootin'."

"Ma!"

Rizzy plods away. Two cubs follow. Lana flops against her seat in relief. Silas tries to start the car. Nothing, and the passenger side is wrapped against the tree. There is no way the wheels could move even if he started the car.

Lana retrieves her phone from the floor of the limo, hands Silas a napkin she found there, and calls Mrs. Badmorn before contacting Triple A.

"What a stupid thing to do," shouts Mrs. Badmorn through the phone. "Silas never tried to avoid an animal before."

"I told him to stop."

"And see where it got you? I should dock your pay for the repairs."

Lana grits her teeth. "If you need to."

"I think I do. Hand the phone over to Silas."

Lana holds her cell phone toward Silas. "She wants to talk to you."

Silas winces rubbing his neck while holding the napkin to his nose. "Shit."

Lana leans back, arms crossed. *Dock my pay? What a bitch.*

***

Walter checks on the pedal boats at the lake. He had managed to buy four good used ones...well, mostly good. Two of them have a blue base with white on top, and a blue shade awning. One is red...was red at one time, but now it's faded to pink with no sunshade. The last one is yellow with a big-ass duck head on the front. The eyes were repainted, giving it a sinister ogle. All of them have two sets of pedals like bicycles. *Good exercise.* Since Kim pretty much fished out the lake, Walter figured the pedal boats would be an attraction. *Damn Dingo's TV ad showed sailboats cruising into the sunset. Idjet.*

"Tyrone!" he bellows and stands, hands on hips, tapping his foot. "Sigh, Tyrone!" No response. If he had a phone on him, he would call the sumabitch. "Stitch!"

"Comin," The distant response. A minute later, Stitch trots up to Walter. He salutes. "Need somethin' cap'n?"

"I need you to gather the campers. We're doin' an activity."

Stitch's eyes practically pop out of their sockets. "An activity? Oh, yes! I'll be right back." He runs off before Walter can say anything else.

Half an hour later, the campers gather to hear about the activity. Senior joins them as well.

Walter bellows while waving toward the boats. "Ladies and gentlemen, today's event is a pedal boat relay race. You will break into two teams consistin' of four folks per team, two folks per boat. Stitch here, will be out there, where you will pedal around him, then back to shore and tag the next group to go. First team wins."

Stitch has both hands over his mouth, then holds his head. "I gotta go out there? You know I can't swim."

Walter gazes up at the sky. "Why me, lord? Tsk, you take the rowboat there."

Stitch swallows. "Right." He stares at the boat like it's going to snap at him.

"Jesus cripes, git out there."

"Oh, man." Stitch drags the decrepit rowboat out into the water. "I don't see a life jacket."

"I didn't git any yet. You'll be fine."

"How do we pick partners?" Tiffany shouts.

"I'll be your partner," Bethany answers sounding like a youngster trying to make a friend.

Walter huffs. "Yer all grownups, partner yourselves up. I ain't gonna do it fer ya."

"What a grouch," Kelly pipes up.

In the meantime, Stitch is struggling with the paddles, flopping them into the water on one side of the rowboat then to the other. He's slowly working his way to the middle of the lake.

Walter shouts toward Stitch. "Stop right there."

Stitch continues to flounder.

"I said, stop right there!"

Stitch stops rowing. "S...sorry, I...didn't hear you," he pants.

Walter moves an arm up in a stop motion. "Stay right there. Drop anchor."

"What?"

"Anchor! Drop the damn anchor. That heavy thing in yer boat."

"Oh." Stitch lifts the anchor and drops it into the water with a splash. "Look, I did it!" His smile wide.

Harley raises a hand. "Do we hafta do it?"

Why do I deserve this? Mother fu... the electricity turns up on Walter's squirrel of a mustache. He rubs it to stop the vibration.

Senior speaks, "No, this is an adult camp. No one is forcing you to do anything but have a good time."

"Is the pool open?" Kelly lifts the hem of her cover-up to reveal a bikini.

For a second there, Walter was afraid she was going to streak naked, or something like that.

Senior raises a brow as if reading Walter's mind. "Yes, Sammy's there lifeguarding."

Kelly waves to Harley. "Come on." And the two head off for the pool.

Walter, hands on his hips, taps a foot impatiently. "Anyone else?" Silence. He does a head count. "Listen, since there are six of you, just team up into three of the boats and go. Screw the relay."

Tiffany is already running to one of the boats, a nice blue one with a sunshade.

"Great idea." Bethany hurries to join Tiffany in her boat.

Tiffany holds out a hand to stop her. "No, you ride with Muffy, and I'll take Kim."

"I ride with Max." Kim waves to Max.

Muffy flicks her hair. "Honey, I believe Max wants to ride with me."

"Um, you girls go ahead. Scottish Bob is with me. Guys against girls, right Bob?" Perspiration beads on Max's brow.

"Aye." Bob smirks.

Kim growls while pointing at Muffy. "You be sorry."

Muffy rolls her eyes. "Jealousy only makes one ugly."

"Screw it, I'm outta here. Jim Beam is callin' fer me." Walter storms off, leaving Senior with the campers.

***

Bethany toddles up to Senior. "What will the winners get?"

Senior's eyes dart about. "Um...uh..." He rubs the penknife in his pocket. An idea comes to him, and he lights up. "A butler! I'll be the winning team's butler for a day."

Bethany jumps and claps. "So, you're already our pool boy for one day, and then our butler for another? We're in."

The girls get into the two good blue and white boats, while the men board the pink boat. Duck boat stays on the bank, the most villainous looking duck Senior has ever seen.

Meanwhile, Stitch opens a bag of chips he snatched from his cabin, and snacks while waiting for the race. It helps to keep his mind off the fact he's sitting in the middle of open water with no life preserver. The three boats line up along the bank. Muffy and Bethany in one, Kim and Tiffany in another, and Bob and Max are in the third.

Senior raises a hand in the air. "On your marks, get set...go!" He throws his arm down.

All pedal with zealous enthusiasm...for about a minute.

"One...two...one...two," Max calls to his partner, Bob, as they pedal in steady unison.

"Get her, get her!" Kim shouts at Tiffany.

Tiffany, being three sizes larger and one foot taller than Kim, puts on the gas in her pedaling to catch up to Bethany and Muffy.

"Muffy try to take my Max. She a hussy. Ram them!" Kim has both hands on the front of the boat as if pushing it.

Tiffany obliges and rams Muffy's boat.

"Hey, cut that out," Bethany shouts.

"You don't own him!" Muffy stands to glare at Kim almost tipping the boat over.

"Sit down." Bethany is pedaling madly, but stops to catch her breath.

Muffy plops onto her seat, while Kim and Tiffany maneuver their boat along her's.

***

By this time, Bob and Max are rounding their pedal boat past Stitch.

Stitch points at the girls, who are now screaming at each other. "What's goin' on over there?"

Bob and Max shrug and continue on their way. Stitch glances up, Kim and Muffy are standing in their boats, both sunshades are broken and flopping in the water. It looks like the ladies are wrestling.

"This is madness. I better get over there." Stitch struggles to pull up the anchor and row in their direction. The oars are awkward, and he abandons one to use the other for both sides of the boat, unaware of the brackets for them. The girls cling to each other as their respective boats float apart.

SPLASH! Kim and Muffy fall into the lake.

"I told you we should have been partners," Bethany shouts to Tiffany. Tiffany is laughing too hard to hear her.

Stitch finally navigates alongside the girls. He holds onto Tiffany's boat while she jumps in and hefts the women back into theirs. She easily returns to hers with a boost. Stitch is in awe of her strength. He had to use about all of his while lifting the dang anchor. Kim and Muffy continue to scream at each other. He doesn't know what to do.

"Cut it out!" Bethany shouts, eyes wide, like an ostrich that's going to peck their eyes out. The warring gals close their mouths at last while Bob and Max disembark from their boat on shore, thus winning the race. "See what you did? Richard Darling Senior is going to be *their* butler for a day. Not us. Noooo, you two had to bicker over Max, who's probably gay. Shoot, he's not even rich. What the heck have you girls learned about men after all these years?"

Muffy hangs her head. "You're right."

Kim waves. "They so not worth it."

"I gave up on men years ago," Tiffany chuckles.

"Can y'all kiss an' make up?" Stitch makes prayer hands.

"I ain't gonna kiss her, but we shake on it...yes?" Kim holds out a hand.

"Yes." Muffy smiles, and they shake hands.

"Thank you, Lawd. Let's get outta here." Stitch begins to row back.

"Feeshin' much more fun than this," Kim says while Tiffany does all the pedaling.

9

WE GOT TROUBLE

At the pool, Kelly and Harley relax on chaise lounges. Samantha is in her lifeguard chair blasting a Taylor Swift song from a nearby Bluetooth speaker.

"Isn't this nice?" Kelly sighs. "It's almost as good as the ad." She leans back on the lounge, closing her eyes.

Harley sits up. "Yeah, okay, but I'm not too keen on this music."

"What? You're not a Swifty?"

"I'm swift, but not into that." He thumbs in Samantha's direction. "Can't she put on some blues, or somethin' like that?"

Kelly closes her eyes, but now they're squinched tight. "It's not so bad. Deal with it."

"You always tell me that."

"Shh! I'm trying to relax."

"Hi guys." Dingo waves to the couple while holding his wife, Miss Pat's, hand in the other. His swim-trunks match his loud Hawaiian shirt.

Harley notices a pineapple printed right over the crotch area. Not that he was looking, but it's a very bright orange illustration.

"Man, that water looks inviting. So, you know, I'm responsible for this gorgeous swimming pool." Dingo removes his shirt. His hairless chest is blindingly white.

Harley nods, feigning interest. "So, you say?"

"Yep, an' I'm the one keeping it sparklin' clean."

"I saw Stitch sweeping it."

Dingo shrugs. "Yeah, sometimes." He waves to Miss Pat. "Come on, Babe." And dives head-first into the pool.

Miss Pat giggles, throws off her cover-up and jumps feet first into the sparkling water. The couple splash each other. Leigh Ann strolls to the pool area in a skirted one-piece suit; a towel slung over her shoulder. Harley wonders why she looks pissed off all the time.

She approaches Samantha. "You took my job."

Samantha turns down the music. "What?"

"I wanted to be the lifeguard."

Samantha leans in toward Leigh Ann. "I thought you wanted to work in the kitchen?"

"Cause I hate teaching crafts. I really wanted to be the lifeguard." Leigh swallows while pushing her glasses back onto the bridge of her nose.

"Sorry about that. I guess you need to take it up with Mr. Darling."

Leigh Ann sniffs, "Whatever." She shuffles to a chase lounge and drapes her towel over it.

Miss Pat swims up to the edge of the pool. "Thanks for switching with me, by the way. I love teaching crafts."

Leigh Ann blows raspberries.

"Tomorrow we're going to paint and sip." A broad smile curls up on Miss Pat's face.

"Sip what?"

"Wine, silly. Mr. Evans went into town and bought wine and liquor to make a bar in the dining hall."

Upon hearing this, Harley jumps up. "Now, that's what I'm talkin' 'bout. Will it be an open bar?"

Dingo lifts himself out of the pool, shaking off water like a dog. "Hell yeah, if I got any say in it." He high five's Harley.

"Drunk old campers," Leigh Ann sighs. "Somebody end my life now."

Junior runs onto the pool deck area toward Samantha. She stands in her chair, surprise and glee on her face. Harley figures those two got something going on.

"Hi!" Samantha's voice sweet as honey.

"Where's Dad? We got trouble, and I hope your legal mind can help us." Junior is out of breath. Sweat pours down his face. He's wincing like somebody stabbed him.

Harley wants to know more. "What trouble?"

"Mrs. Badmorn fired me."

"What'd you do?"

"Nothing! She's closing Caring Souls and kicking out the residents."

Samantha's brows knit. "She can't do that."

"That's what I said, then she had Lurch, I mean Silas, kick me out." Junior frantically points toward the nursing home. "Some of them already got picked up by their families because the hag told them the home has to close down because the state made her. She lied, and now, folks are in there with no place to go."

Dingo joins the conversation. "Shit, no tellin'."

Junior grabs Dingo by the arm. "She said we're next."

Dingo steps back, mouth agape. "Nooo, she can't do that." He glances up at Samantha, still standing in her lifeguard chair. "Can she?"

"Only if there's outstanding property tax that hasn't been paid."

Dingo swallows. His face reminds Harley of a kid called to the principal's office. "Oh, damn. We need to talk to Senior."

Harley approaches his wife, Kelly, who's sitting up at attention with a *what's going on?* look on her face. He sits next to her and nods toward Dingo. "Seems like trouble in paradise."

***

Cases of beer, wine, and liquor bought by Walter are being unloaded by Stitch and Chef Fry in the dining hall. Nurse Oyomama checks on her list of campers for what types of liquor will interact with medications.

"How ya goin' to supervise their drinkin'?" Chef Fry asks while placing beer in the refrigerator.

The nurse answers in her Jamaican accent, "I will send notes to ta darlin's lettin' tem know what's safe."

The chef chuckles, his belly jiggling under his apron. "Oh yeah, that'll work."

Nurse Oyomama blushes and laughs.

Walter is standing in the doorway checking off boxes as they are carried in. "It won't be no problem. Seniors know their limit. It's damn kids who have no control."

Chef Fry squints one eye at Walter. "You sure 'bout that?"

Walter waves the comment away.

Senior strolls up to him, forlorn, with both hands in his pockets. "So, I guess I'm going to be butler for a day, and a pool boy."

"Heh, that's your problem, buddy."

"You took off on me. It was nuts out there, and they wanted some kind of prize." Senior pulls his hands out of his pockets to rub his eyes. "I didn't know what else to do. I can't believe two old...I mean, adult women would fight over Max."

Walter smirks. "Who else, you?"

"No! I mean...you should have stayed. It was your big idea."

Walter drops the clipboard to his side, and he's face to face with Senior. "In case ya didn't notice, this here is a summer camp. Git it? Summer camp. You have dumbass activities. That's what summer camp is for. Any more questions?"

Junior, Dingo, and Samantha rush into the office.

"Dad!" Junior trips over a crate of liquor.

"Watch it!" Walter shouts. "That's good stuff there."

Ignoring Walter, Junior jumps up. "Dad, we got trouble. Serious trouble."

Senior is calm and waves him off. "If it's Mrs. Badmorn, I got her number. She isn't a threat. So, she built a road? So what?"

Walter growls, "She took my woods."

Dingo nudges Junior aside. "It's worse than that!"

"What now?"

Junior pants. "Remember when I left all those bills on the desk?"

"An' when I took off to Vegas?" Dingo adds.

Senior eyes both men. By now everyone is surrounding them, listening in. "Yeah...so?"

"So, we're screwed, and it's all my fault! I took that money. It was stupid...stupid! I'm so sorry, man." Dingo runs a hand through his shoulder length wet hair.

Junior wraps an arm around Dingo's shoulders. "No, it's mine. I didn't pay any attention to where the money went." He wipes tears from his eyes with the back of his hand.

Senior throws his arms out in confusion. "What the hell is going on?"

"Mrs. Badmorn is kicking everyone out of Caring Souls and plans to take this camp too."

"Oh, really, and..." Senior's hands are now on his hips.

"Samantha told us Badmorn could take Sedation Falls if the property taxes aren't paid." Junior sniffs, "I'm so sorry, Dad."

Samantha hugs him.

"Me too!" Dingo sobs.

Senior plops onto his chair at the desk and holds his head in both hands.

Walter's wooly-bear mustache quivers. "What a bunch of sorry ass idjets."

"This is bad, Walter. She got us on this one."

Walter struts to his desk, pulls open a drawer, and holds up a piece of paper with the word *PAID*, stamped in red on it. "You talkin' 'bout this? Confound it, man. It was the first thing I did when I agreed to help run this shithole."

Everyone cheers, rushing Walter to hug him. "Back! Back, I say."

Samantha laughs. "He's not a hugger."

The muscles throughout Senior's body turn into limp noodles with relief. He takes his lucky penknife from his front pocket and kisses it. The joy is short-lived though as Junior recounts to everyone about being fired, Caring Souls residents sent away, and how the ones who are left are being treated like prisoners.

"It's not legal," Samantha explains. "And by the time it takes to go through the courts, those remaining residents could die."

"Where will she take them?" Senior asks.

"I don't know." Junior paces. "She'll have that Frankenstein monster, Silas, drop them somewhere bad, I know it."

Nurse Oyomama steps forward. "Tey can come here."

Senior gasps. "We don't have room."

"How many are still there, love?"

Junior counts on his fingers. "Five."

"We can do it, Mr. Darlin'." Nurse Oyomama places a hand on Senior's shoulder. "You will be a hero."

It's not being a hero that concerns him. Senior wonders how the paid campers will appreciate five more in their midst, and where will they sleep?

"I have room for two in my cabin." The nurse raises two fingers like someone bidding at auction.

"I ain't takin' no old fugitive in my cabin," Walter grouses. "Scottish Bob is enough."

"I can sleep on a cot in the kitchen. The bunk bed kills my back, and Dingo snores like a wild pig," Chef Fry volunteers.

"Shit, really?" Dingo shuffles his feet. "I'll sleep in my truck then. Been doin' it for months now anyways."

"There ya go." Stitch rolls up his sleeves showing no muscle tone in his skinny arms. "I now have room fer three. I don't mind sharin' my futon."

"I'll go bunk with Max." Senior sighs. "And Junior can sleep on the cot in the office."

"So, I gotta squeeze past his ass?" Walter slaps his hand on his desk.

"Guess so," Junior answers.

Nurse Oyomama claps her hands. "T'en, it's settled. We rescue the residents."

"How?" Senior asks. "Mrs. Badmorn hates us. She won't let them come here out of spite."

10

BADMORN

Mrs. Badmorn sits in the office of Caring Souls Adult Center. She is dressed in black mourning the death of her husband even though he passed months ago. It was actually a relief to her because for the whole sixty years of their marriage, he had control of their finances. He kept giving the money away to charities, making it impossible to keep up with the Goodnights, and when they built the Umstead Hotel, that was the last straw. She was more than happy with the purchase of Caring Souls Adult Center to facilitate care the last few months of his life, and saw it as the perfect location for her own Spa Hotel once he was gone. It will surpass anything the Goodnights own.

Beverly Badmorn, nee Webster, dropped out of college her freshman year to the relief of her parents. Mother and Father didn't have the finances to get her through, and her high school grades weren't even close to getting a scholarship. Beverly decided the only way to get ahead was to find a man with money, so she got a job at a golf clubhouse. The wealthy love to play golf and they like to drink. She was a server at the Nineteenth Hole, and that's when she met Barry Badmorn—a millionaire. It was love at first sight...for him. He was ten years older than she with a face you would miss in a crowd, but he showered her with attention and lavish gifts. Best of all, no family to worry about. He was an only child whose parents died of lung cancer. Apparently, both of them were big cigar aficionados. The estate left to him was enough to start his own business creating yellow pages directories. It made him millions.

When the internet took over, Barry turned to an online directory service. Beverly had respected his mind...and his money. Now, it is her turn. With the investment in Caring Souls and soon, Sedation Falls, she will have the best spa hotel in the eastern U.S., far surpassing The Umstead. She'll call it the Instead Hotel.

A *tap tap* on her door. It is her last staff member, Margy. She enters the office carrying a box. "I got the meds, C-Paps, and some other stuff here."

Beverly Badmorn nods in approval. "Are they ready to go?"

"Yeah. Want me to give this stuff to Silas?"

"No. Just set it down. He'll get it. Your severance will be in the mail."

"Crap," Margy mumbles.

"Pardon me?" Mrs. Badmorn sits up, one eyebrow raised.

Margy sighs. "Okay. You got my application for the spa? I'm good at massages."

Mrs. Badmorn nods, waving Margy away. "Go on, now. Tell Silas we're ready."

Margy walks out the door while giving Mrs. Badmorn the side eye.

After waiting several minutes for Silas, Mrs. Badmorn loses her patience and swings the door open. Rizzy towers over her. Silas is motionless beside the rental van he picked up after the accident.

Margy is standing next to him. "I'm out of here. That bear can have her." She strolls to her car, salutes the scene and drives away.

Rizzy growls, baring her teeth. Beverly Badmorn grimaces, showing her teeth. "Shoot it!"

Silas reaches into his jacket for his gun. "It's too close to you!"

Rizzy roars.

"Go away bear. Go away. Shoo!" Mrs. Badmorn calls.

Rizzy gets down onto all fours shaking her head vigorously.

"Nice bear, go away now," Beverly instructs with a calm voice, but she actually wants to smack it and tell it how dare it startle her. She reaches for the doorknob and slams the door shut. "Shoot it," she screams from inside. "Do it. Now!"

BANG!

Silence.

Relief floods over her and she opens the door once again. The hind end of the bear enters the woods. Lana is now standing next to Silas.

Mrs. Badmorn storms toward the two. "I told you to kill it!"

"She has cubs," Lana defends.

"Lana pushed me. Doesn't matter though, we scared it off." Silas thumbs toward Lana. "Next time, I'll make sure she's not around."

Lana remains stone-faced, sunglasses on, leopard bag slung over her shoulder. "Pretty sure it is illegal. Besides, the bear can make it a good case to take over Sedation Falls. How can they run a senior citizen summer camp with bears running amok?"

Mrs. Badmorn claps her hands in glee. "Good thinking. That is why I hired you, Lana. You are always one step ahead. Excellent." She straightens her mourning clothes. "Well, let's get these cronies loaded up."

Silas holsters his gun. "Where am I taking them?"

"Anywhere. Drop them off at some farm for all I care. I'm sure there are lots of public shelters to take them to. Figure it out. Maybe Lana has an idea?"

Lana adjusts her sunglasses. "How about Sedation Falls?"

Just the mention of that place makes her blood boil. It's going to cost her a lot of money to get rid of Richard not-so-Darling Senior, jackass Junior, wacko Walter, and dumbass Dingo. Her eyes narrow at Lana. "These seniors don't have the money to give to the camp, do they?"

"No. Their funds are only to go to physical care, not recreation."

Beverly tilts her head in thought. "Hm, that camp is already busting at the seams." She squinches her face to resemble a baby. "Thay wouldn't turn down poor wittle helpless old folks now, would thay? The grey-hairs left here have no family that want them. That should tell you something about how hard it is to manage them, right?"

Lana nods in agreement. Silas strolls inside to gather the residents. After a good twenty minutes, which is twenty minutes too long to Beverly, Silas comes out with five residents in front of him. He pushes one of them. "Move it."

The man, Wilson, spins around to face Silas. He brushes wild long frizzy white hair from his eyes. "Don't touch me, or I'll have ta lay ya out!"

"Whatever. Get in the van."

"A van, aye? What happened to yer limo? Oh wait, I remember, you wrecked it."

"He wrecked?" One of the women, Meredith cries.

"Yeah, an' we're s'posed to get in yer rental van to God knows where? Yer nuts."

Silas gives him a hard shove. "Get in the fuckin' van!"

"What about our luggage and medicines?" Meredith asks.

Mrs. Badmorn steps into the conversation. "They will be delivered to your new homes. You all have nothing to worry about. Everything is under control."

Wilson raises his fist into the air. "Why believe you? We know what you're doin' and it ain't legal."

"Poor Will needs his meds before dinner." Meredith points toward resident Will, being lifted with his walker by Silas into the van.

Mrs. Badmorn lets out a long sigh, goes into her office to retrieve the box of supplies. The sooner she gets these sorry losers out of here, the better. She storms out and shoves the box into Meredith's arms. "Here! Happy? Now, get in the damn van."

Wilson stands firm in front of the van's doors. "You're all up to no good!"

Silas draws his gun from his jacket and points it at Wilson.

Wilson clicks his tongue. "Well, if you're gonna put it that way, I guess I'll go." He stops on the step of the van and glares at Silas. "Cause I believe you'd really shoot me."

Silas nods. "Correct. You'll be dead soon anyways."

11

SILAS

Silas drives the van containing the Caring Souls refugees down the smooth, newly paved lane, straight through the middle of Sedation Falls summer camp, but there's something going on in the road ahead. It looks like they're playing a game. As the van nears, he can tell the end of the drive has been turned into a Pickle Ball court and old folks are playing.

"Now what?" Silas stops the van, opens the door, and reaches for his gun, when a huge shape fills the door's opening. He's struck in the face, gun knocked out of his hand, and pulled outside. It's Chef Fry. Silas is big, but Chef is huge. When Silas struggles to his feet, Chef Fry knocks him back down.

"Tie him up, tie him up!" Stitch is jumping up and down.

"Get him! Get him good," Bethany shouts.

Silas is woozy and can't get his grounding. His arms are pulled back, and wrists tied together by Senior.

Chef Fry drags Silas to a tree and props him against it. Samantha and Leigh Ann help the Caring Souls residents out of the van.

Walter picks up a branch, pulling the leaves from it. "Where are ya takin' 'em?" He smacks the branch on the ground like a whip in front of Silas. "Where?"

Silas isn't afraid of these old farts, but a whipping by a big angry geezer with the bushiest eyebrows he's ever seen could hurt. "Here, dumbass."

"Here?"

"Duh!"

"I heard Badmorn tell him she doesn't care where he drops us off." Wilson gives Silas a kick.

Walter thwacks the branch in his hand. "Is that right?"

"Sure. She doesn't give a shit about any of y'all."

"That bitch!" Mildred stomps.

Walter scrunches one eye at her. "Mildred? I thought you flew off to Cali."

"I changed my mind. My family didn't really want me there. I liked it here until...HER."

"Here, love." Nurse Oyomama hands Mildred a Kleenex and she dabs at her eyes with it.

Richard Darling Senior spreads out his arms to the homeless bunch. "You are welcome to stay with us."

Nurse Oyomama retrieves the box of supplies from the van. "We made room for all of you."

Mildred claps her hands. "This is lovely. I've always wanted to stay here."

"What about me?" Silas growls. The rope is burning his wrists.

Senior unties him.

Silas rubs his sore wrists. "You're all a bunch of assholes."

Chef Fry steps forward, fists balled, ready to punch. "What did you say?"

"Let me at 'im!" Mitchell, the fifth Caring Souls exile shakes his cane, limping toward the woods instead of Silas. Mildred takes him by the arm and guides him to the group.

She nods to Nurse Oyomama. "Cataracts—he can't see well."

He shakes his cane once more. "I can see fine. I was just makin' a loop."

"You know? You all may think you're heroes right now, but it ain't gonna last long. You're gonna lose this stupid place." Silas glares at the group for a dramatic pause. "One way or another."

Bethany waves him off. "You go on home now."

"And be sure to tell the lady to kiss my fuckin' ass." Walter's mustache seems to be growling instead of him.

"Walta'!" Scottish Bob shakes a finger at him.

Walter's bushy brows arch high. "Oh, yeah. She's not a lady. Tell the witch to kiss my mother fuckin' ass." His mustache curls up into a smile.

Bob shakes his head and sighs.

Silas has had enough of these clowns and strides to the van. He points at the Pickle Ball court. "And get rid of this. You're on Badmorn property." He reaches into the van, retrieves his sunglasses and pats his jacket. No gun. He holds a hand out. "Give me my gun."

"This?" Stitch holds the dissected gun in his hands and strolls over to Silas. "Sorry man, I was tryin' to clean it for ya. Kinda got carried away."

"Argh!" Silas grabs the pieces of his nine millimeter, gets into the van, and revs it while performing a three-point turn around with it. *We're gonna make them sorry.*

When Silas returns to Caring Souls, Mrs. Badmorn is packing up boxes. "That didn't take long." She hands Silas a box. "Here. Put this in the van." She points at packed boxes on the floor. "These too."

Silas begins to head out with a box when Mrs. Badmorn asks, "Were they thrilled to receive the extra campers?" She smirks.

"Actually, they tied me up to get them. A big black guy punched me."

"What? What a bunch of idiots. Next time, we'll just shove them out of a moving car. I guess that would be better." Mrs. Badmorn titters, seeming to enjoy the thought.

Silas carries the box toward the van. *She didn't even ask me if I was hurt. Bitch. She doesn't pay me enough for this shit.*

As he loads the last box, Lana drives up the lane. She eyes the van. "What's all that?"

"Don't know, don't care. I'm taking her to pick up the limo. It's ready."

"That was wild, wasn't it?"

"When they tied me up?"

"What? I was talking about the bears. Who tied you up?"

"Those stupid campers down the road. I was droppin'
off the rest of the codgers, when I was accosted."

"You dropped off the rest of the Caring Souls residents there?"

"Yeah, it was your idea."

Lana smiles. "I didn't think she would do it, though."
She reaches into her leopard print bag, retrieves her
sunglasses, and puts them on. "Listen, please do me a
favor. If you see those bears again, don't hurt them.
Okay?"

Bleeding heart liberal. "If it comes down to them or
me, it's gonna be me. I'm just sayin'." Silas waves while
getting into the driver's seat.

12

BOOM!

"You two lovelies will sleep in my cabin." Nurse Oyomama nods to new arrivals Meredith and Mildred, while still carrying the box of supplies.

Stitch jogs up to her. "Here, Ma'am, that looks heavyish. I'll take it for you."

Nurse Oyomama hands the box to Stitch. "This is Tyrone, a sweet 'art, he is."

He nods to the women. "Call me Stitch."

"Oh, I already met him." Mildred covers her mouth with a hand while giggling.

"Rule number one, Miss Mildred, stay out the bathhouse." Stitch's pure sunny smile lights his face.

Mildred raises her right hand. "I promise."

The nurse and Meredith cock their heads in confusion.

***

"Here's your cabin." Dingo opens Tyrone's cabin door to escort new campers Wilson, Mitchell, and Will with his walker inside.

"A bunk bed?" Wilson is agog and wrinkles his nose while placing a hand on the top bunk. "I hate bunk beds...especially when the guy above or below me farts." He thumbs toward Will. "And this guy farts to keep himself upright."

"Not true." Will shakes a fist at him.

Dingo strides to the front of the cabin where Stitch's futon is placed in front of the TV. "Someone can sleep on this too, but you'll have to share it with Stitch. But, no worries, he's skinny as linguini, so there's room."

Wilson shakes his head, causing his long, grey wildman hair to fall in front of his face. He blows the strands away. "I don't like to share."

"Don't know what else to tell you, man. We're filled up. I'm sleeping in my truck."

"Trade ya."

"Naw, that's okay."

Wilson's eyebrows tilt up in a pitiful countenance. Combined with his unkept hair, it's quite a pathetic look. "Well, shit, I'll sleep on the floor then. I'm used to the pain in my poor arthritic hips." He stretches with a hand pushing against one hip.

Dingo gazes at the ceiling and sighs. "Good, I'll get ya an extra blanket for cushion."

***

The next morning, campers shuffle into the dining hall for breakfast. Walter is on one side of it stocking up the bar. It is old, with bleach stains all over the countertop. Stitch is helping Mitchell to a seat at a table when he notices the familiar storage cabinet.

He approaches Walter. "Where did this come from?"

Not looking up from unboxing liquor, Walter says, "The shed by the pool pump."

"You mean, this is the thing we keep the chlorine and pool chemicals on?"

Walter stands, his mustache at attention. "That's right. It ain't just a thing, it's a bar. It needed a lil cleanin' up is all."

"A little?" Stitch sniffs the top of the bar and squinches his face.

"Yeah, a nice, clean smell."

Stitch shakes his head and begins to walk away. There is nothing he could say to get Walter to stop this madness.

Walter calls out to him. "We're havin' a big to-do tonight to welcome our rookies."

Mildred is eating breakfast nearby, when she lifts her head, eyes wide. "Rookies?"

Walter sighs and bows to her. "I mean new folks, okay?"

Mildred nods and continues to eat.

Stitch does a head count of people at breakfast. "Anyone see Mr. Wilson Bitner?"

"He left the cabin last night," Will calls. "He took a pillow and blanket and said it was none of my concern." He shrugs. "You were already asleep."

"Shizzlesticks, I betta' look for him."

Walter asks, "Want me to call Senior?"

"No, no, I gots it." *Why me, Lawd...why me?*

***

Stitch is searching the property when he spies a blanket crumpled up on top of a picnic table in the pavilion.

Grey and black gnarly fur of some kind is peeking out from under it. It appears to be some kind of animal, like a racoon's tail? It moves. Stitch jumps back, stifling a scream. *Wild animals scare the bejesus outta me.* He searches around and finds a fairly heavy branch. He holds it like a baseball bat while approaching. It sits up.

"Aaaah!" Stitch screams, dropping the branch.

"Mornin'." The animal is Wilson. He scratches his head, his crotch, and his armpits.

Stitch stares, blinking.

Wilson stretches. "Ahh, best sleep in years."

"Why didn't you stay in my cabin?"

"Hell, and deal with Mitchell's snorin' and Will's farts? No thank you."

"Oh."

"Shit, kid, you sleep through anythin'." He spreads out his arms. "I got me the perfect spot here."

Stitch rubs his chin. "I guess there's no harm, 'cept I think a bat was nestin' in your hair."

Wilson chuckles while patting down his mat of mane.

Muffy strolls by on her way to the pool wearing a two-piece swimsuit. The bottom is a flowered skirt, and the top is neon pink with a big ruffle across her breast. She has her dyed blonde hair up in a ponytail that swings back and forth with every step.

Wilson bobs his eyebrows. "Woo, that suit clings on all the right places. What's her name?"

Why me, Lord...why me? "Uh, we call her Muffy."

Wilson watches her walk by. He jumps off the table wearing only a pair of aqua boxer shorts, places his fingers in his mouth, and whistles a long loud wolf call. "Muffy girl, you are on fire!"

She turns and waves with her fingers as though playing a piano and giggles before going on her way.

Wilson claps his hands. "I got a pool to get to."

He begins to stroll away before Stitch stops him with a gentle grip on his arm. "You should get dressed first, sir."

Wilson glances at his shorts. "Oh, yeah. Good idea."

***

The atmosphere at Camp Sedation Falls is jovial as Walter sells a steady supply of beer and wine. Everyone is at the pool laughing and having a good time. The eight-foot Tiki god, Kane, that Dingo bought last year with Senior's money, stands smiling wide at the deep end, just beyond the diving board.

"That yer bike over there?" Wilson asks, while nodding toward Harley's cabin.

"Yeah, it's a twenty-twenty Honda Goldwing."

The men are sitting on the edge of the pool. Wilson straightens his back when Muffy swims by. "I had a Harley myself...a Road King Classic. I rode it on the Iron Butt tour."

Harley's brows float up from the middle. "Oh, really?"

Wilson raises his voice so that Muffy will hear. "Oh yeah, Sturgis, Daytona...you name it. In fact, I completed the Butt Burner Fifteen Hundred."

"Wow."

"Yeah...and I did it all AFTER I retired." Wilson lowers his voice and leans in toward Harley. "I guess a Harley was out of your league. I mean, why else would a guy named Harley own a Honda?"

Harley grimaces and leans back. "I like Hondas. They're a hella better than fuckin' Harleys."

Wilson raises a palm to Harley. "Whoa, man. Didn't mean to insult you."

"Smooth ride, an' never a breakdown."

"I hear ya."

After a few beats, Harley thumbs toward his bike. "Wanna go for a ride?"

Wilson stands, "Hell, ya."

Harley rises to his feet. "Then, let's go."

The two men stroll past the pavilion where Miss Pat is teaching Kelly, Tiffany, Bob, and Mildred how to paint a picture of a beach. Three empty bottles of wine sit on a picnic table as Miss Pat pours from another bottle into her students' glasses.

Harley pats Kelly's back. "Hey, Wilson's gonna ride the bike. We'll be right back."

Kelly holds her painting up. "Look, isn't it cute? I didn't know I could paint."

There is a seagull in the picture that, given proper proportions, would be big enough to swallow everyone at camp. "Yeah, looks good."

She crosses her brows. "I know when you are lying."

"Damn."

She smiles and returns to her work. "But that's why I love you."

"Whew."

"And Mildred," Wilson calls.

Her work interrupted, Mildred glances up, giving Wilson the raspberries.

Wilson lifts both thumbs in the air. "Lookin' good."

"Oh, God, shut up." She fumbles with her paint.

As the men continue on toward the cabin, Wilson thumbs over his shoulder. "She's into me. Never seen such a crush."

Harley chuckles, shaking his head.

"Are you married?"

"Kelly and I have been together for twenty years, so, I call her my wife."

Harley nods his head in agreement. "Yeah, I'll never get married. I don't like to be tied down."

"Aren't you like, seventy-five?"

"Seventy-six, so?"

"So...never mind." Harley places his hand on his motorcycle.

"Here she is."

Wilson leans over to study the motor. "Nice. Looks like a lotta cubic inches."

"A hundred and twelve."

"Yeah, lotta horsepower there."

"Yep."

An audience has gathered, Kelly, Mildred, Stitch, Bethany, Tiffany, and Walter. Muffy is approaching wrapped in a towel. Wilson swings his leg over the seat. Harley tosses him the key.The motorcycle is a lot larger than Wilson expected. His toes barely touch the ground as he strains to level the bike.

"You okay?" Harley asks, "If it's too big, we..."

"Naw, man," Wilson quickly answers. Muffy is here. He can't back out now and look like a pussy. He can tell she likes real men. "I got this." He turns the key, pulls in the clutch, presses the starter button, and revs the engine. He pats the back seat. "Hey, Muffy girl. Wanna ride?"

She smiles, tight lipped while shaking her head, *no*.

"Later babe," Wilson grins maniacally. He lets out the clutch while cranking the gas. The bike pops forward, stalls, and falls over, along with Wilson. Luckily the roll bars on the front of the bike prevent him from being crushed.

Everyone runs up to him. Wilson lies on his back, one foot under the bike, the other splayed on top. His eyes are closed.

"Is he dead?" Muffy pants, out of breath, after rushing to the scene.

Stitch runs up to him while clutching a spoon. He blows on it and rubs it dry on his pants, then holds it in front of Wilson's nose. He checks the back of the spoon. There is condensation. "Naw, he still breathin'."

"Where the hell you git the spoon?" Walter grouses.

"I was eatin' breakfast."

"Still eatin' breakfast? Holy Cheerios."

"We gotta get my bike off the guy." Harley strains to lift his motorcycle. The others pitch in to help.

The bike now righted; Wilson's eyes stay closed. Stitch shakes his shoulder. "Are you all right? Anything broke?"

Walter stomps. "Jesus Cripes, he better not be hurt, damn it. That's all we need."

"I'm okay," Wilson answers meekly, eyes still closed. "I...I never rode a Honda before."

Harley nods, hands on his hips. "Yeah...so..."

"So," Wilson swallows. "I never rode any bike. I just read about 'em."

Muffy's hand covers her mouth to stifle a laugh.

"Son of a..." Harley kicks dirt near Wilson.

"Sorry about that."

Nurse Oyomama runs to the scene, holding bandages in both hands. "Step aside, let me treat this man." She begins feeling Wilson's arms and legs for any swelling or breaks. She begins to massage his stomach and chest for internal injuries.

"Hm, that feels good." Wilson leans forward onto his elbows.

Nurse Oyomama jumps to her feet glaring down at him.

"Nothin's broke, 'cept for my pride."

"Good thing you didn't give him mouth to mouth." Stitch pockets his spoon and helps Wilson to his feet.

"That woulda been even better." Wilson winks at the nurse.

Nurse Oyomama huffs, taking her bandages back.

Wilson wipes off his pants and approaches Harley. "Is yer motorcycle okay? I'll pay fer any damages, I promise."

"It's fine," Harley answers, "Just a bent footpeg. Easy fix." He chuckles. "See what happens when you let your mouth work harder than your brain?"

"Or your libido." Kelly laughs.

"Oh, right. Ha. Ha." Wilson avoids looking at the group...especially Muffy. She must believe he's a total idiot by now.

A chilly breeze blows as dark clouds roll by. The group breaks up to return to their cabins.

Walter places a hand on his chest. "I don't need no more emergencies like that. Damn idjet coulda broke somethin'."

Kim and Max strut over the hill hauling a string of trout. "We caught dinnah!"

Walter rubs his mustache. "Wow I thought you had that lake all fished out by now."

Kim stands her whole four feet-eight inches. "If there is feesh, we git 'em."

Max pats her back. "That's right, Doll."

The couple go arm in arm toward the dining hall.

"Doll?" Walter raises an eyebrow.

Thunder rolls in the distance. Drops of rain fall.

"I need to get to my chapel before the storm."

CRACK...BOOM!

A bolt from nowhere strikes yards away from him. The clouds release a downpour. Walter gazes up at the sky. "Fine, fine." He shakes a finger. "Later!"

***

Campers run into the dining hall. There is nothing to do trapped in their cabins during the storm, so they make their way to Walter's bar.

BOOM!

Stitch jumps. "That was close! Dang, I hate storms. They make me jumpfergus."

"Jumpfergus?" Walter asks.

"Yeah, jumpy and nervous."

KABOOM!

Stitch jumps. "Dang!"

Walter slaps him on the back. "You need a drink."

"But I'm not twenty-one yet."

"Son, I saw you mixin' drinks. You don't fool me."

Stitch snickers while shuffling his feet. He holds up a finger. "Welp, jus' one."

A bright flash of light snaps through the windows. Stitch grabs Walter for protection. CRACKLE...BOOM!

"Let's git that drink." Walter peels Stitch away from him.

Senior bursts into the dining hall. "Caring Souls is on fire!"

13

LUBRICATION

Everyone rushes to the window. A crimson glow breaks over the hill. Sirens soon fill the air. Firetrucks speed past the camp.

"Holy Toledo." Walter's mustache curls into a smile. "Good riddance to bad neighbors."

"Lightning musta hit it." Stitch gawks, eyes wide.

Bethany slaps Walter's arm. "You better pray nobody was inside."

"At least we were all out, but I don't know about Mrs. Badmorn." Mildred leans against Bethany to get a better view of the glow.

"Dad," Junior calls. "We should go over there."

"You're right." Senior moves toward the door and stops. "You all stay here." He waves to Stitch to come over to him and whispers, "Entertain them."

Stitch salutes. "Okay, boss."

Senior and Junior dash out the door. Leigh Ann shuffles up to Stitch. "What now?"

"I dunno."

"Hell, I know one thing," Walter bellows. "This calls fer a drink." He holds up a glass of whiskey. "On the house."

The campers belly up to the bar while Walter pours. Stitch wrings his hands. "Oh, Lawd."

***

Pulling up toward Caring Souls Adult Center they are stopped by the influx of fire engines, police cars, and an ambulance. Senior lurches out of the car and runs up to a paramedic. "Is anyone in there?"

"We don't know yet."

As the men watch the center go up in flames, Mrs. Badmorn's limo pulls up. Silas exits the driver's side, strolls to the rear passenger door, and opens it for Mrs. Badmorn and Lana. None of them appear to be upset. They're cool as cucumbers. All three gaze at the blaze as though watching marshmallows toast. A heat of his own builds inside of Senior. He faces Mrs. Badmorn. "You don't care, do you?"

Her demeanor doesn't change. She wipes a fleck of ash from her jacket.

Silas glares at Senior, his one hand is balled into a fist while the other one holds an umbrella over the women. "Back off, asshole."

"It's alright, Silas." Mrs. Badmorn nods to him. "Mr. Darling, this is none of your business. The place was empty. We were just beginning the remodel. What a shame." She tsks.

"Come on, Dad. Let's go," Junior calls from the car.

Senior turns to find himself face to face with Lana. His heart skips a beat, and he tells himself to stop it.

"We need to meet," Lana says with her sultry throaty voice.

Stop it! "Why? I'm not selling Sedation Falls."

"We have a new offer...one you can't refuse."

Those lips...stop it! Senior is sweating in the cool mist of the receding storm. Silas is still glaring at him. Mrs. Badmorn seems rapturous while watching the fire. Her eyes glisten in the light, a Mona Lisa smile on her lips.

"Where?" Senior wants to smack himself.

"Your turn." Lana purrs.

"My office." *I should be safe there.*

"Tomorrow? Say six? We can get dinner after."

Senior does his best to appear nonchalant and waves her off limp wristed. "Yeah, sure."

"Dad!"

The suddenness of Junior's shout makes Senior jump. His son nudges him aside to face Lana. "It doesn't matter what you say...or DO. The camp ain't for sale. Ever!" He pulls on his father's arm. "Come on, Dad. Screw them."

Senior feels like a kid tempted by a new toy, but his papa said, "No".

While Junior leads him away, Lana nods to Senior. "Till tomorrow."

Senior nods slightly, and when his son isn't looking.
***

Meanwhile, the campers at Sedation Falls are being well lubricated by Walter.

"What are we gonna do now?" sniffs Leigh Ann.

"Cripes, I don't know." Stitch runs up to Samantha. "Get your granddaddy to stop servin' booze."

Samantha throws her arms up in frustration. "I tried. He said he will when he runs out."

"Dubdoggone, what are we gonna do?"

"I know," Muffy shouts and giggles. "Let's have a fashion show."

"Huh?"

"The guys wear the girls' clothes, and the girls wear the guys!"

Wilson sidles up to Muffy. "Wear the guys? I'm in." The back of his hand rubs against her backside.

She steps away from him laughing. "No, silly. I mean the guys' CLOTHES."

"I'm still in for that, baby." He unbuttons his shirt, exposing a very furry grey chest.

Muffy begins to unbutton her blouse.

Samantha rushes to place a hand over Muffy's. "Wait, wait, not here! Tell you what. It sounds fun but go to your cabins and we'll give you outfits for the show. Sound good?"

The campers laugh and nod.

"This is madness," Stitch whines.

Muffy buttons back up. "It'll be fun."

Wilson's bottom lip pokes out like he lost a puppy. "Change in our cabins? Tsk, fine."

Bethany bumps into Samantha and plops into the nearest chair. "There is no way I can get back to my cabin in this con...contrition. I'll fall."

Walter pushes Wilson aside, his mustache curled in disgust. "Keep yer shirts on, got dang it!" He turns to Samantha, palms flipped up. "We need an activity right now before they all go off into corners to screw or spew."

Samantha steps back in surprise. "Grandpa!"

Stitch doubles over in laughter. "Screw or spew. You got that one, boss."

Walter waves a hand toward Muffy. "Nobody's changin' clothes. Just go model what y'all got on an' I'll commendate."

"You mean, commentate?" Samantha asks.

"Yeah. That's what I said!" He pulls a chair from a table. "Help me set this up. We're gonna call it "Who the Hell Goes to Sedation Falls?"

"Grandpa...really?" Samantha clicks her tongue while helping him arrange the seats.

Chef Fry brings out a roll of meat packing paper to drape down an aisle between the chairs creating a runway. As campers sit, Leigh Ann passes around a tray of Ritz crackers and cheese. Nurse Oyomama hands out bottles of water.

Wilson holds up one of the bottles. "I ordered a beer."

"We ran out of beer, my love." The nurse opens his water. "Dis will help your hangova."

"I never get a hangover."

"Good for you, den."

Walter saunters to the front of the hall and raises his arms for silence. "Everybody here?"

The campers and counselors glance around, shrug, and mumble.

"Great. Welcome to our first Camp Sedation Falls fashion show. We have several victims...uh, volunteers exhibiting only their finest camp attire." Walter swings an arm out toward the group. "Our first model is none other than Muffy. Muffy, come on down."

A smattering of applause. Muffy flips her blond ponytail and strolls along the butcher paper catwalk in pink pedal pushers and a gingham blouse.

Walter continues, "Yes boys, this cutey is a throwback to 1963—the time of muscle cars and Miss Clairol."

Muffy giggles. "That was the year I was born."

Walter's mustache curls into a sneer. "Only her hairdresser knows fer sure." He waves. "Next up is Tyrone, but we call him Stitch. He has a funny way of sayin' shit."

Stitch strolls along the catwalk, chest out. His skinny legs poking from the hem of his khaki shorts remind Walter of two brown paper straws sticking out of empty toilet paper rolls. The toolbelt hanging from his narrow hips holds the entire collection of Craftsman tools, and he carries a plunger like a scepter. He sashays and spins.

"Let's lend a hand to our own maintenance man."

Stitch holds the plunger high. "You got a clog? Call me, I'll suck that mess right out." He bats his eyes.

Walter clears his throat and guides Stitch along pushing on his back. "Alright then. He's very dependable."

Stitch spins, waiving the plunger. "You can count on me to git at it day or night!"

Leigh Ann snickers. Walter hears her. "Right, right...uh, Leigh Ann. Come on down."

She shuffles along the walkway wrinkling the paper, eyes darting one side of the aisle to the other. She does not smile, but her permanent scowl fits her. She sniffs, pushing her glasses back onto her nose. Leigh Ann is wearing black jeans and a black T-shirt. The ensemble she wears every day.

Walter bows to her. "Counselor and kitchen helper, Leigh Ann...a Wednesday Adams wanna be."

"How did you know?" she mouths.

"Bet you played Dungeons and Dragons...a lot."

Leigh Ann's brows arch high. "How did you know that one? Wow, you're good."

"Yes, I am. Now, move along." Walter shoos her on. "Next up, we got the amazing fashion sense of Wilson...if we were living in 1953," he scoffs.

Wilson bows in his lime green with white stripes bowler shirt and black short shorts. A pack of Camel cigarettes peeks out from his breast pocket. He has the countenance of a smug actor. "Thank you, thank you very much."

Walter tilts his head, studying the outfit. "Are yer shorts short enough?"

"They are in style. I realize it's way after your time, sir. They show off my tan and keep my balls in check." Wilson turns a shoulder to dismiss Walter.

"Huh, not only are yer balls in check, but I think they went AWOL."

Wilson lifts his chin uppity. "You, sir, are jealous." He swaggers along to the applause from the women in the audience.

Walter pets his quivering mustache. "Move along, I'll tell Daisy Duke she won't get her shorts back." He bows. "Ladies and gentlemen, we must not miss our newest and youngest campers, Harley and Kelly."

The couple stroll out wearing their motorcycle gear, jeans, and black leather boots. Harley is wearing a dusty blue baseball cap with the visor curled to resemble a duck's bill. Kelly's hair is pulled back in a ponytail, and her head is wrapped in a black and orange Harley Davidson bandana. Kelly bats her eyes at Walter. "Thank you, but we're over fifty."

"So are we. Way over fifty."

Kelly continues to the end of the paper aisle and does a turn wearing her navy blue Camp Sedation Falls T-shirt. The neck opening has been cut to a V, revealing her décolleté. Outstanding nipples poke at the fabric. She has shredded the bottom hem of her shirt to create fringe waving in the breeze, exposing her bellybutton. There is a collective gasp from the audience. "I can do up these shirts for you ladies if you like."

The men applaud.

"So, Kelly," Walter taunts "What's with the bandana? You ride a Honda, not Harley."

"Heh." A sly grin grows on her face. "Yes, I do ride Harley."

Walter at once regrets asking the question. It suddenly feels very hot under his mustache. So hot, he could shave it off right now. He picks up a bottle of water and chugs it down.

"Oh yeah, baby, I got a Harley to show ya!" Harley takes Kelly's hand, and they jog out of the dining hall doors.

Walter sighs, patting down his mustache. He clears his throat. "Now, where was I?"

"Me! Me!" Bethany waves.

Oh boy, here we go. "Okay, okay. Without further ado...Bethany." Walter's mustache droops as much as his head while stepping aside for Bethany.

She tip-toes onto the paper catwalk, pirouetting and giggling. She's wearing a green beach cover-up bedecked with huge yellow flowers Walter figures she got from a clown when the circus left town. A shocking pink swim-suit peaks out above the collar. Bethany is carrying a beach bag larger than her ass in the crook of one arm. Her face is shaded by a wide-brim straw hat.

Walter sighs. "As you can plainly see, she is ready to take a swim...or at least a chair by the pool to gossip."

She waves him off. "Oh, you..."

"You better take sunglasses to protect those ostrich eyes of yours."

Bethany stops, hand on her hip. "You think you're so funny. I got them right here." She reaches into her bag and pulls out a pair of round sunglasses that make her eyes look buggy instead of beady. "So there." She struts to the end of the aisle and sets the bag down. She grips the hem of her cover-up and begins to pull it off.

Walter waves with both arms. "Stop, stop!"

"Doncha want to see my suit?"

"No! No, that's okay. We don't wanna turn on the whole place now, do we?" He takes her elbow to guide Bethany to her seat.

"Oh Walter," she blushes. "I knew you have a thing for me."

Walter releases her arm. "I gotta thing fer you all right. It's called a fly swatter."

"You're funny," she titters and stands there.

"Uh, move on." Walter waves.

She leans in toward him. "Pardon me?"

"Go on, now. We got more models."

"Tehe, he called me a model," Bethany giggles while prancing to her seat.

"My turn," Dingo calls out.

Walter's grin is more of a sneer. "Here is your 'Florida Man' mascot, Dingo."

Dingo trots onto the catwalk wearing his typical Hawaiian three-sizes-too-small shirt. The buttons strain most at the acme of his belly, yet his cargo shorts are three sizes too big, the hem falling below his knees. He's wearing sandals, but his tan stops at his ankles where he had been wearing socks. Dingo takes Miss Pat by the hand to walk with him. She's wearing a loose Moo-Moo dress that would hide the shape of a Goodyear blimp. It reminds Walter of a bell. Her tiny legs would ring it.

Walter eyes the couple up and down. "You two need to talk to yer stylist."

"I wear my shorts loose to let my boys roam free." Dingo stands proud, hands on his hips, pelvis thrust forward.

"And I let my girls roam free." Miss Pat cups her breasts.

Walter steps back. "Good God, you two better not go to Florida after all."

Miss Pat flutters the hem of her dress to cool her lady parts. "Oh? Why not?"

"Cause a gator'll come along an' chomp yer boys and girls right off!"

"Don't knock it till you try it, Walt." Dingo scoffs.

"It's Walter."

"Whatever." Dingo guides Miss Pat on to their seats.

"Damn idjets," Walter mumbles and straightens. "It's not a proper summer camp without our professional fishermen, Kim and Max."

"Fisher people!" Kim shouts. She steps onto the catwalk wearing her floppy khaki fishing hat, army green capris, navy blue camp shirt, yellow rubber gloves that go all the way to her elbows, and she's barefooted.

Walter's caterpillar brows reach for the sky. "Damn, last time I saw gloves like that it was on the farm to impregnate cows."

"Not cows...feeshing!" Kim pantomimes sticking her arm under water. "Find feesh inna hole." She mimes a fish grabbing her arm and raises it while flopping about. "I git beeg one." She mimes holding a big fish. Max is standing nearby with a fishing pole. Other than that, he appears to be the most normal model in the show with his khaki pants and Camp Sedation Falls T-shirt.

"She's cat fishing," Max answers, deadpan.

Walter raises a brow. "And what are you fishin' for...compliments?"

"Oh, ha, ha, Walter. You must be a graduate of the school for the chronically obtuse comedians." Max guides Kim arm in arm to their seats.

Walter's not sure if he's just been insulted. He's heard of obtuse in math. Something about angles. "Uh, thanks."

"Psst, Walter." It's Senior peeking at Walter from the door of the kitchen. He and Junior have just returned from the Caring Souls fire. Walter strolls over to him, and they whisper to each other for a few moments.

Walter returns to the group while clearing his throat. "Well, well, well. We have a very special guest." He throws his arm out toward the kitchen. "Let me introduce, Lana, Mrs. Badmorn's lacky."

Senior wobbles out of the kitchen toward the paper catwalk teetering on Muffy's high-heeled shoes. Cat-eye sunglasses frame his face. He has on a short pink skirt revealing hairy unshaved legs, and carries a burlap potato sack cut like a purse. He sashays the best he can, his fuzzy toes squeezing out of the shoes, and swivels to pose. He imitates the sound of a phone. "Brring, brring." He reaches into the bag, pulls out a potato, and holds it to his ear. In his best high-pitched female voice, "Hello? Oh yes, I can buy that...uh huh." Pause. "An' that, an' that, an' that. Oh, he'll be a piece of cake. I got him all sewn up, honey. No man can resist me." He taps on it.

Wilson stands at his seat and cups his mouth. "Yeah, baby!"

Senior pretends to be coy, batting his eyes and puckering his lips. He holds the potato to his eye. "Smile for the camera, suga'."

Walter grimaces. Wilson poses. Everybody laughs.

Senior continues the charade, pointing his potato camera at the campers. "Click, click, cli..."

He looks up. Lana is standing at the door of the dining hall, red faced and fuming.

"Uh, oh."

She storms out.

Walter shouts to Senior, "She deserved it." But he can see by Senior's face, that the man's heart won't let her go.

14

A CURE FOR HANGOVERS

Wilson is lying on top of a table in the dining hall. He's snoring louder than Rizzy's growl. Bethany nudges him. "Hey, get up. We need this table for breakfast."

Wilson jerks his head up and moans. The pain in his head jackhammering the back of his eyeballs. He holds his forehead with one hand and lies back down.

Bethany gives him a hard shove. "I said, we need this table for breakfast!"

"If'n you say, breakfast, one more time, I'm gonna hurl." Wilson slowly makes his way to a seated position, squinting. It appears to be some crazy bird he's looking at.

Bethany crosses her arms. "So, you never get a hangover, huh? What a sight."

He realizes it's Bethany pecking at him, but it doesn't matter. Wilson closes his eyes and moans. Last night's dinner is threatening to make an encore. He swallows it back.

"Go see Nurse Idoyou Oyomama."

"I do you, or your mama? Not now, I have a screamin' headache."

"No, dummy, I mean Nurse Oyomama. She has the cure for hangovers."

"Oh." Wilson edges off of the table onto his feet. He tries to focus on Bethany, but there's two of her...and she's weaving all over the place. *Wait, that's me doin' the weavin'.* His hand snaps to cover his mouth as he lurches to the nearest trash can and throws up into it.

Bethany's voice behind him. "At least you made it to the can, but you have to clean up that over-wash."

"Huh?" Some of his puke has splashed out, but he doesn't have the strength to clean it. Wilson stumbles out of the hall in search of the nurse.

When Wilson arrives at Nurse Oyomama's cabin, there is a line waiting to see her. A bucket is passed up the queue to spew into.

He spies Muffy there, and Walter. Muffy is two people ahead of him. He calls her. "Hey, hey Muffy."

She turns around without moving her neck. She smiles weakly. "Hey."

"Some line, huh?" Wilson pats his frizzy bed head down.

"Yes, Nurse Oyomama has the cure. We'll be fine by this afternoon."

"Oh yeah? What is it?"

"Some Jamaican drink blended with pickle juice, ginger, hot sauce, and peas."

Wilson staggers out of the line and heaves. Since he's already lost the contents of last night's dinner, most of the vomit is neon green.

Walter cringes away from the splash. "I better not step in it, or I'll tan yer ass."

Wilson's shoulders droop. How embarrassing to puke in front of Muffy. "Sorry." He gets back into his place in line in spite of the grumbling from others behind him.

***

Junior is putting away the cot he slept in, while Senior broods at his desk. "Wow, Dad, you shoulda seen Lana's face watching you at the fashion show."

Senior nods a slow sad acknowledgment. "Yeah, I can imagine by the way she stormed out. I don't even know why she was here. We had already made an appointment to meet. She said Mrs. Badmorn has some offer we can't refuse."

Junior stops what he is doing and glares at his father. "See? That woman is mafia. She won't give up until we're dead. She'll probably burn our camp down like she did with her place."

"Now, don't jump to conclusions. Lightning most likely hit it."

"Yeah, right. Dad, they're playin' us. Psh, we can refuse any of their offers." He pushes the folded cot into a corner with a bang. "It's easier to build a whole new place with the bundle of insurance money ol' Badmorn will get. That storm was the perfect time to do it."

Senior runs a hand through his hair. "Damn."

A knock on the door. It's Max and Scottish Bob.

Senior signals for them to enter. "Hi guys, how can I help you?"

"Do you remember the peddle boat race a week ago?" Max asks.

Senior shrugs, "Yeah."

Bob shuffles toward Senior's desk, stops, and leans on it with both hands. "Do ya nae 'member ta prize?"

Senior leans back in his chair. "Yeah, but I..."

Max points to himself and Bob. "We're the winners. You said you'd be our butler for a day."

Senior squinches his eyes in thought. "I guess it was something like that."

"That day be taday." Bob's hand covers his heart. "We be recoverin' from de evils of liquor. We canna rest twhile our butler serves us."

"Yeah." Max sits at Walter's desk. "And you promised to be the girls' pool boy, remember?"

Both of Senior's palms flip up toward the ceiling. "But I have an appointment today."

"It's with that buyer, Lana." Junior sounds like he's talking about a spider. *It's with that spider, Lana.*

Max looks up from snooping at the papers on Walter's desk and smiles, "Well, that won't take long."

Walter fills the doorway with his presence, "Git the hell away from my desk!"

Max jumps up and hustles to stand next to Bob at Senior's desk.

Walter brushes his seat off with a rag. "I heard what y'all were jabberin' about. Go be their butler chump. I'll handle Lana."

"But..."

"I'm a partner, remember? I'll take Junior with me. You go serve these old, sick men."

"We're not, we're just…" Max thrusts an accusing finger at Walter. "You saw us in line. You got a hangover too!"

Walter sits, organizing his paperwork. "Yeah, I drank the Kool-Aid an' I feel much better now." He leans toward Senior, bushy brows headbutting. "An' thanks fer askin'."

Senior sighs, eyes rolling up toward the ceiling. "It was your idea to have a bar."

Walter rubs his head. "Huh, you gotta point there."

Scottish Bob slaps Senior's desk. "So, it's settled, den."

Senior scratches his head. "I guess."

"We'll be at the pool." Max turns to leave and stops. "Oh, and please bring us towels and I would like a virgin Bloody Mary."

"I'll take a scotch on da rocks." The others stare at Bob in surprise. "Hair of da dog, do ye ken?"

***

Walter and Junior make sure they are in the office at six p.m. for Lana's arrival.

Walter is writing at his desk. "No matter what she or her dingle-berry boss promises us, the answer is, no."

Junior takes a seat at his father's desk. "Right, but she's got us surrounded."

Walter continues writing with hard, sharp strokes of the pen. "We're gonna make HER an offer she can't refuse. Those woods are mine…and Rizzy's. I won't let her fuck 'em up."

"You go, man."

"I'm glad it's us meetin' her. Leopard-bag-lady would bat her eyes at Senior, and he'd flop onto his back like a damn pup waitin' on a belly rub." Walter gathers his papers, tapping them onto the desk to straighten the pile.

An hour later, there is no Lana, and the dining hall is oddly quiet. It should be full of campers by now finishing their evening meals. Finally, there is a knock at the door, but it is Chef Fry. "Suppa is cold. Where in Jesus is everybody?"

15

A SEMBLANCE OF SANITY

Walter stands, his fuzzy brows spark. "Good question. Where the hell is everyone?"

A high-pitched whistle belonging to no bird Walter has ever heard, pierces the air.

Junior's arms fly up, his eyes, wide. "What was that?"

Walter, Chef Fry, and Junior, stand silently in place, listening.

"Yee haw!" A cheer echoes from the direction of the swimming pool.

Junior runs to the doorway the same time as Chef and both squeeze together to get outside.

Walter rolls his eyes. "Damn idjets. What'd Senior git himself into this time?"

As the men approach the pool area, Muffy and Wilson are making out in the pavilion. There is a ball being thrown around in the water with no real sense of rules. A group of four is seated at a small table playing some card game. One of the men removes his T-shirt. Stitch is there running back and forth, legs kicking high in the air, while screaming, *stop this madness, stop this madness!* Scottish Bob is strolling around the edge of the pool wearing a kilt and banging on a drum.

Walter is relieved to find a semblance of sanity in Max, who is sitting calmly. That is until Kim lies on a lounge chair and lifts her shirt. Max pours a shot of Tequila into her bellybutton and leans over to suck it out.

Junior stands in shock. "Oh, my God!"

"Oh, boy. This ain't my scene. See ya." Chef Fry turns and stumbles back toward the dining hall.

Walter finally spies Senior. He's pushing Nurse Oyomama's medicine cart, but it's not medicine he's dispensing. Tiffany, who is in the water at the edge of the pool, places her finger and thumb into her mouth and whistles. The intensity of the pitch assails Walter's ears. She holds out a red Solo cup. Senior lifts a pitcher from the cart, pours her a drink, and moves on to the card players, while being followed by Nurse Oyomama yelling at him to give it back.

Harley is whistling and shouting while throwing a ball in the pool at other campers. It appears to be a game of dodge ball. He throws it at Tiffany, hitting her in the shoulder.

"Cut it out! I almost dropped my drink," she screams.

One of the card players, Mildred, unbuttons and removes her blouse, revealing breasts packed into a bra two sizes too small. Senior picks up the blouse with the tips of his fingers and holds it to her, trying in vain to get her to put it back on.

Samantha is seat-dancing in her lifeguard chair with her Bluetooth blasting *Margaritaville* by Jimmy Buffet.

This is the last straw. Walter sucks in a huge load of air in order to boom out with, "That's it! Everybody out of the pool!"

The partiers freeze. Samantha snaps off the music. Silence, until Harley emits a long, low, belch.

"What the f...son of a monkey's ass is goin' on?"

Richard Darling Senior begins to step away from the cart toward Walter. Nurse Oyomama snatches it. He swivels from Walter to her. "I had to use it. I couldn't manage all those drinks myself."

"You mean booze. Toes folks need medicine. Eats all my fault. I ne'er should ta geeven tem my elixir. Tey feel too good now." She begins to check over her cart, when she grabs a baggy of gummies. "An' what is tis?"

Senior holds out both of his hands, spreading the fingers wide. "Candy?"

Walter points. "That isn't mine."

"Arg!" The nurse throws the baggy into the pool and dumps the liquor from her cart, pouring the contents of each bottle onto the grass while searching for the medicines.

Wilson has left his make-out session and moves to stop her. "Hey, hey, hey, that's good shit there."

Walter blocks his path. "Don't think 'bout movin' one more inch, buddy."

Senior slaps himself in the head. "Oh, man, it all got out of hand. One minute I'm Max and Bob's butler, and the next thing I know, I'm serving everyone."

Scottish Bob approaches. A gust of wind catches his skirt. Walter is relieved the man is wearing swimming trunks underneath. "Tis my fault. I told 'im to, as...as my butla'." Bob rubs his neck.

Mildred sheepishly buttons up her blouse.

"What?" Harley climbs out of the pool, the soggy baggy in one hand. "This was gettin' to be my kind of camp." Kelly hands him a towel.

"Listen up." As Walter glares at everyone, his woolly brows nearly covering his eyes, he is a stark opposite of tiki God, Kane, with his wooden smile forever laughing at the scene. "This is a Senior Citizen camp. We can't be responsible for the death of a camper who partied too hard. Your families think our idea of partying is S'mores by a campfire, an' that's what we're by Jehoshaphat gonna do."

"Party pooper," Bethany mumbles.

Walter's brows go into full-on wrestling match. "Yer damn right." He dips one neck- wrenching nod.

Nurse Oyomama approaches. "Dey need food."

"Yep, it's cold, an' I'm not tellin' Chef to warm up the spaghetti neither."

The group mumbles in dissent while making their way down the hill toward the dining hall. Junior and Samantha help the woozy ones walk. Three men appearing to be in their 50s, break from the group and head toward the parking lot.

Walter shouts after them. "Who are you?"

They don't answer, and instead, mount their motorcycles, revving them. Harley taps Walter on the shoulder. "They're my buddies."

Walter stomps his foot. "No more company. This place is for paid campers only!"

Harley lifts his palms to the sky. "Okay, okay...sheesh!" He lopes with Kelly down the hill toward the dining hall and holds her hand.

Senior rubs his eyes. "I thought you said Seniors were mature enough to monitor their own drinking."

"I said *I* could." Walter bends over and picks up a cream-colored double D brassiere—extra coverage. "They can if'n ya don't let 'em run ripshaw over ya."

Senior's eyes grow large at the vision. Walter tucks his fists into the cups of the bra. "You let 'em bamboozle ya, Kemosabi."

"Who does that belong to?"

Walter holds it up, fists well hidden in the cups. He studies it. "Don't know, but she's my kind o' woman." His carpeted brows bob up and down.

Senior snatches the bra and tries to shove it into the pocket of his khaki shorts. It doesn't go willingly and hangs halfway out. "You know, I...well, Dingo and I bought this camp thinking all we had to do was fix it up a bit, sit back, and collect the money. My mother wasn't anything like these people. She was happy to sit in her room all day and watch soap operas. What's wrong with Seniors these days?" He plops onto the bench of a picnic table and runs his hands through his hair.

Walter saunters up to his friend. "Was she ever asked what she wanted?"

"I...I don't remember..."

"She prolly had no say in the matter. The folks we got here ain't gonna sit around all day. They plan on livin' till the livin' runs out."

"I'm sorry," Senior sniffs, "Lesson learned."

"Hey, did you see leopard-bag-lady? She didn't show up at the office."

Senior sits up, blinking. "Lana? No."

16

WHERE'S LANA?

Richard Darling Senior strolls the remaining property of Sedation Falls. It's been a few days since the booze debacle. The campers seem to have recovered well, thanks to Nurse Oyomama. She's forgiven him for appropriating her cart for alcohol. It was dumb of him but got himself wrapped up in an effort to make everyone happy.

Walter and Stitch gathered the group around the campfire last night and made S'mores, just like Walter promised. It was a big hit. Walter reminds Senior of a S'mores sandwich—crusty on the outside, gooey and sweet in the middle. Although Walter would never confess to it. Of course, he had to tell one of his off-color jokes, like the one about the lonely old man who got drunk and bought himself a blow-up doll. She flew out the window when he nibbled her neck, taking his false teeth with her. Senior slaps himself on the forehead and smiles, *where would we be without ol' Walter?*

Senior walks past the swimming pool. A few folks are relaxing on lounges. Miss Pat is teaching an art class in the pavilion. Stitch made sure to sweep out any bugs or spiders that may have inhabited the space. The ladies have drinks beside them—sweet tea, except for Kelly. She has a glass of wine. *Good here.* He moves on down the hill toward the dining hall. Chef Fry is preparing ribs on an outdoor grill and Leigh Ann is actually helping him.

Next to the hall, a group is playing pickleball on the new road Mrs. Badmorn had built. One of the players, Stitch, is running around after the ball. "Stitch!" Senior calls, hands cupped to the sides of his mouth. "You're not supposed to run in pickleball."

Stitch holds up a paddle, just as a whiffle ball flies past it. "They're makin' me." He turns to the players. "Where y'all learn to do this?"

Senior chuckles and moves on. There is no sign of Walter. Senior figures he snuck into his chapel in the woods for some...he makes quote marks with his fingers, "meditation". The weather is a perfect mid-seventies on this late July morning. Senior stretches and sighs, *I wonder why Lana never showed up. She said she had an offer I couldn't refuse. Maybe she got smart and figured I wouldn't take it. "An offer I can't refuse" my ass.* He begins to head on to the dining hall for a cup of coffee when the sound of heavy machinery crunching over gravel severs the bliss of a peaceful day.

Three construction vehicles' brakes squeal to a stop in front of the pickleball court. The window of the truck in front of the parade rolls down. The driver leans out. "Move it. You're in our way!"

Wilson, one of the players, flips him off.

Senior marches toward the truck driver, signaling, *go around.* "There's a drive off of 421."

"We were told to come through here." The driver thumbs behind him. "I got lumber to drop off and a tight schedule, so tell the assholes to move!"

Stitch plops cross-legged in the middle of the road. Wilson and Muffy do as well. With great effort and noise, Bethany sits on the ground with them. All glare at the driver defiantly.

The driver talks into a cell phone. The ruckus attracts the attention of other campers. Senior and Harley grab lawn chairs and place them on the road for those who can't get to the ground. The scene gives Senior a warm feeling in his heart. These people love this camp. The sit-in is a perfect statement of it. He joins them and sits crossed-legged on the ground.

"We ain't movin' till you do!" The driver shouts.

"Neither will we!"

As the minutes pass, Senior is joined by the rest of the counselors and campers. Within an hour, everyone is there, except for Walter. *He may have fallen asleep after smoking his pot. Or maybe he's gathering a posse' to save the day.* Senior rubs the penknife in his front pocket and prays these guys will turn around and leave. The worst people to show up would be Lana and Silas. *That limo could be rolling up any minute, but I don't care. This is MY camp.*

BANG! BANG! BANG!

Gunfire. Campers scream and scatter.

HONK! The truckers lay on their horns.

Bethany is rolling around on the ground. "Help, I can't get up!"

Tiffany and Stitch runs to her aid.

BANG! BANG! BANG!

The group duck and scream. With a blast of effort, Tiffany pulls Bethany to her feet.

Senior grabs Stitch. "Get everyone to safety!"

The counselors guide everyone toward the dining hall, heads down.

BANG!

All make their way for safety...except for Wilson. "Where are they? I'll kick their asses!"

The trucks start up and roll onto the road. Wilson begins to run toward them. Senior has to pull him away. The rigs run over the pickleball net and several chairs.

"Son of a ..." Wilson shouts.

Senior's heart is racing, and he struggles to catch his breath. "Stay here. You could get killed. We'll get to the bottom of this, but not now."

"Call the police!"

"I'm sure someone has."

BANG!

Senior pushes Wilson. "We got to get to safety."
***

Walter is sleeping in a rocking chair in his chapel in the woods until gunfire startles him awake.

Silas, Mrs. Badmorns' driver, is approaching the clearing, holding a pistol, shooting in the air. He spies Walter and shoots. The bullet flies over his head. Walter freezes in place afraid one of those will hit him if he moves.

Silas points the gun directly at him. "What are you doin' in Mrs. Badmorn's woods?"

"This here is my place. I don't give a rat's ass what it says on paper!" Walter isn't sure if it's adrenalin or a heart attack he's feeling, but by gum, he isn't going to take flak from anyone—armed or not.

The rustling of leaves causes Silas to pivot toward Walter's right.

Oh no, Rizzy! "Rizzy," Walter shouts, "Go back!"

"Ma." The plaintive cry from one of the cubs.

17

RIZZY!

Rizzy's Story

I was abandoned at a young age; only two years old, and never knew my father. My mother left while I was hibernating in our den. I had been asleep, and couldn't tell how long she was gone. I searched everywhere for her and wandered through the forest, frightened and hungry.

Berries were good, but I needed something more substantial and the thought of killing another animal was repulsive, gross, and messy to me. After ambling for miles, exhausted, and ready to give up, the aroma of warm and savory filled my senses and made my mouth water. Small humans all wearing the same coverings over their hairless bodies were grouped around a fire. Yummy looking things were hanging on the ends of sticks hovering over the flames, sizzling and popping. I edged closer in hopes one of those humans would toss me one, but instead, cried out, "Bear!"

I ran back into the protection of the woods and watched. A large human ran up to the small one. He had a light torch and shone its beam toward my shelter. I ducked away from it.

"C'mon, boys—nothing to be afraid of. We share our woods with all sorts of wildlife, especially bears. The bears around here are called, Black Bears. They mean no harm, but I wouldn't pet one. Smokey the Bear they ain't, heh, heh."

The small humans moaned like they had pain somewhere, then followed the large human with their sticks to what he called, "cabins". I waited until it got dark and scuttled toward the cabins when my nose picked up the divine scent. Drooling uncontrollably I ran toward the source, losing all sense of fear, and that's when it happened. A pitchfork thunked the ground in front of my muzzle. Sliding to a stop, I fell and cried out.

"Well, I'll be a monkey's uncle. You're just a skinny little thing," the large human said. "I'll be right back." He ran into the cabin the smell was coming from. I didn't understand what he said, and it made me sad. I rolled into a ball and closed my eyes; so close to finding food.

"Hey, bear!"

The human returned. I cowered, not sure what he was going to do. Several of the small humans, still dressed the same, ran up behind him. "Hi, bear." They waved. Their faces weren't showing teeth in anger. Their mouths were turned up...happy. It made me happy too.

"He's skinny."

Understanding the word "he", I chuffed, *I am not a he,* but they didn't seem to understand.

"Hey, boy, want some hot dogs?" The large human held out a handful of brown things that looked like fish, but they had no fins, tails, scales, or eyes. He called them "hot dogs". They laughed as I caught them in mid-air. Those "hot dogs" were so good. It was the best day of my life.

Every evening they fed me "hot dogs", strawberries, marshmallows, fish, the occasional steak, and ice cream sandwiches. As I grew, I learned to do tricks for more food; sit and beg, fall on my back and play dead, or wave with one paw. When the summers were over, I would go to my den and sleep. Then every new summer, a crop of small humans wearing the same coverings over their hairless bodies would arrive.

One summer they were gone. I waited every evening, but no one came. There was no aroma of "hot dogs". I couldn't wait any more. Starvation led me to the cooking cabin. I pushed open the door and clawed my way into the silver metal box that held them, only to find small bits of food remaining and licked it clean.

Berries and acorns became my diet. I was a vege-tarian—until that sweet aroma crossed my nose again. "Hot dogs!" I hurried to the cooking cabin. The door was open, and stepped in believing the nice humans had re-turned to feed me, but no. These humans screamed and threw things at me. A fish was on a counter all dead and clean, so I snatched it and ran.

Those humans were not nice...until I met him, the hu-man with a bushy face other humans called, "Old Coot". He walked right into my woods, rolled dry grass into a little white leaf, and lit it on fire. He called it "smoking". Humans are strange, but I must admit it smelled good. He talked to me like I was a friend, and even called me

Rizzy. He brought me "hot dogs". It was nice having a human friend again. I did tricks for him, and he smiled like the small humans I once knew. Old Coot saved me when ticks burrowed behind my ears. I couldn't swipe at them and he picked them off for me.

Like the other humans, he went away at the end of the summer. A month later, I met a strapping, handsome male bear. After a whirlwind romance, he left. Just like that. I gave birth to two cubs to raise by myself. When Old Coot returned, I had to show him my new family. He came into my woods often for smoking. I sat for hours watching him while the cubs played. Old Coot talked to me and sometimes blew the relaxing smoke toward me. I always felt mellow afterward, even when my cubs got too rambunctious. I owed him, and vowed to protect him and the other humans who don't wear the same coverings over their hairless bodies.

Now's my chance. I can smell a bad human a mile away, and this one is pointing a bang stick at Old Coot.

***

A blurred shape to Walter's left bashes against Silas. He stumbles and drops the gun. It fires. Silence. For seconds, until Rizzy thunders through the brush on Walter's right. She rears up onto her hind legs and pushes Silas down. He howls. Rizzy growls, baring her teeth.

A high-pitched scream. It's Lana. She was the shadowy figure that hit Silas. Now, she's at the edge of the clearing, eyes wide, stark terror on her face.

"Git the gun!" Walter shouts, wresting out of his chair.

Lana breaks from frozen fear and snatches the gun. She fumbles with it in her hands.

"Calm the fuck down." Walter makes his way toward the melee. "Rizzy won't hurt you." He points at Silas splayed on the ground underneath the bear. "Just him."

Silas shrieks. Rizzy roars, drool dropping onto his face.

Walter takes the gun from Lana. "I got it from here."

"Ma!"

Rizzy's two cubs emerge from the safety of the woods and step into the clearing. They appear unharmed. Walter pats himself. No blood. *Whew!* The bear slowly moves away from Silas. Her cubs scamper toward her. Silas remains flat on his back as one of the cubs approach his feet. It sniffs his shoe, then sneezes. Mama bear nudges her cub aside. Rizzy sits on her haunches considering Lana.

"It's okay, Rizzy girl. She's a friend." Walter continues to point the pistol at Silas.

Rizzy snorts, rises, and lumbers back into the woods—her cubs trotting close behind.

Silas sits up. Walter notices a distinct wet spot on the guy's pants around the crotch area. "You'd piss yourself, too," Silas shouts.

"I almost did."

Silas turns his attention to Lana. "What the fuck, Lana?"

"You were supposed to scare them away, not shoot them!" She crosses her arms. "That's it. I'm done. I can't take this shit anymore."

"Tell the boss that." Silas begins to stand.

Walter waves the gun at him. "Stay right there, bud, till I figure out what to do with you."

Sirens in the distance. Beads of sweat break on Silas's forehead. "Listen, man. I had no intention of shooting your ass. I was just doin' what I was told. If you let me go, I promise I won't do it again."

"No?" Lana stands askant. "Promise you won't tell her about me?"

Silas glares at her.

"Lana," Walter begins, "Go wave those cops down..."

"Fine! I promise. Please, let me go." Silas rubs a thigh.

Walter shrugs and lowers the gun. "Why not? I don't know how to use this thing anyways."

Silas jumps to his feet and lunges for the pistol.

Walter points it at him. "But I'm sure it's easy to learn. I pull this here trigger, right?"

Silas turns on a heel and runs into the woods.

Lana swings her arm in his direction. "The limo is parked over there."

Walter cups a hand by one ear and listens. The sirens stop. "And so are the police."

Lana stands, blinking back tears. "Are you going to turn me in?"

Walter limps to a wooden pew in his chapel. Arthritis is cracking nuts in his knees, while pain in his side is a pronghorn ram butting against it. Too much excitement for one day. He sits and ponders a moment. "Hm, I have ta think on it. You did save my life...fer what that's worth."

Lana seats herself on a nearby stump. "I hate to admit it, but he was taking aim at one of your bears...not you."

"Rizzy?"

"Rizzy's cubs. He would kill a helpless animal without any hesitation. I couldn't let him do that."

Walter's bristly eyebrows lift in surprise, resembling two alarmed porcupines. A smile creeps underneath his mustache. "My kind o' gal."

Lana's shoulders relax and she laughs.

"I almost didn't recognize ya without yer big ol' leopard bag."

Lana lifts a finger in the air for Walter to wait. She jogs to the edge of the clearing and steps into the woods. A few moments later, she appears with her bag. "There's no way I would leave that behind." She reaches into it while walking back, pulls out her cell phone, and eyes the screen. "Yep, there she is. Ol' Mrs. Badmorn calling." She drops the phone into it and smiles crookedly.

Walter rubs his knees. "Heh, aren't ya at her beck and call?"

She swings the purse over her shoulder. "Uh, no. Especially since she..." Lana shakes her head. "Never mind."

"Listen." Walter adjusts his seat on the pew. "Will ya do me a favor? Can ya hand me my backpack?" He points to his pack lying on the ground next to his rocking chair. Lana picks it up and hands it to Walter. He deftly opens it and rummages a hand around inside of it. "So, you and wanna-be-gansta Silas were out here to scare us away?"

She sits on the stump, places the leopard bag on her lap, and nods. "Something like that. I...I did something stupid. I was angry Senior made fun of me at that miscreant fashion show. I was supposed to offer two mil for the camp, but I told Mrs. Badmorn it was turned down. I knew her next move was going to be big, but…" Lana wipes a tear from her eye with the back of her hand. "This was only one play in her chess game. She's hiring a team of attorneys to prove you've broken laws about caring for Seniors here."

Walter snaps to attention. "What?" His backpack slides from his lap, but his hand firmly holds onto a baggy of marijuana. "What in Sam hell you talkin' 'bout?"

"A bunch of issues. Someone got trapped in the bathhouse, plying Senior Citizens with alcohol, almost drowning them in the pool, no lifejackets on the peddle boats, encouraging bears…"

"Stop right there, sis." Walter leans forward glaring at Lana. "We didn't break no damn laws."

"Her attorneys will twist it to look that way…and I must say, it won't be hard."

"I can't believe I told Rizzy you're a friend. Why I oughta…"

Lana stands, holding her bag in front of her chest. "I am a friend. This is all my fault. I'm sorry. Mrs. Badmorn is more of a bitch than I am."

Walter's anger disappears in a puff of smoke, and he laughs.

"I promise you I will do everything in my power to stop her." Lana continues, "She's dangerous. I don't believe her husband died of natural causes. She could have Silas kill one of you to prove your camp is unsafe." She strokes her hair away from her face with both hands. "I'm a buyer, not a murderer."

Walter can't process all this new information without a cleansing toke of weed. It'll calm him down and allow him to think straight. Without a word, he leans over, retrieves his bag, and brings out a pack of rolling papers.

Lana's head tilts while reading the label aloud. "Rizzola?"

"Yeah, I named Rizzy after 'em." Walter begins to roll a joint.

"After rolling papers?"

Walter stops and scowls at her. "Yeah, an' I got a doctor's permit fer this. Wanna see it? Huh? Ya gonna sic the law on me?"

Lana window wipes with a hand while shaking her head. "No, no, I was just asking a question. Can we call a truce? Please?"

Walter's shaggy brows bob up and down. "Like over a peace pipe?"

She smiles and nods.

"Well, I ain't got no peace pipe."

Lana's shoulders droop, along with her smile.

"But I got some peace pot." Walter places the joint between his lips and lights it.

18

BREAKIN' THE LAW

Lana is standing next to Mrs. Badmorn observing the trucks demolish what is left of the Caring Souls Adult Center. She's in her usual uniform of a shift dress, hair in a bun, and dark sunglasses. Her leopard purse is hanging from her shoulder. "It's a shame."

Mrs. Badmorn, still wearing a black mourning dress asks, "What is?"

An excavator is picking up wooden rubble and dropping it into the bed of another truck. A bulldozer is pushing metal debris into a separate pile. Lana waves an arm toward the remnants. "This. Building your spa from the ground up. That center had good bones."

"Good bones? Hah! Maybe a few skeletons in the closet, but good bones?" Mrs. Badmorn winks. "My dear, the storm was the best thing to happen to that dump."

Lana puckers her mouth and removes her glasses. "You didn't consider it a dump when your husband was there."

Mrs. Badmorn turns on her cane to face Lana. Her jaw set firm. "Oh please, do I have to detail the facts of life to you? Or, how about a math lesson? Not only do I have the freedom to make my own decisions now without his interference, but I have a nice fat account to play with. His illness was sucking it dry. Hopefully, I will have enough time on this Earth to make the Goodnights bow at my feet. They will look like hobos next to my estate."

The ridiculousness of her statement causes Lana to question her own role in all of this. She spent her adult life detaching herself from feeling any empathy toward owners of properties sold out from under them. It was their own fault for allowing those properties to go into foreclosure. She is merely a representative for those buying, and she makes a healthy commission. It's smart.

For the past few years, being a purchaser for the Badmorns obtaining property legally...or not, and often with strong arm tactics have given her pause. Then it was the bears. Her fear when Silas was willing to run over a cub and kill Rizzy. She can't believe someone would be so eager to end the life of a living being, until realization punches a hole into her hard core. *Why, I'm no better than them. I lured Richard Darling Senior to bed in hopes he would sell, and it was MY idea. I've been ending livelihoods. I'm...I'm just as bad.* With the fog in her brain for the past five years clearing, she curses her apathy for the humans whose lives she ruined. Lana replaces her sunglasses to cover the tears welling in her eyes. "Do you have a will?"

Mrs. Badmorn's hand rests on her hip. "Of course I do!"

"Is any of it going to charity?"

"Are you trying to be funny?"

"I...I think the Goodnights sponsor charities."

"Fine for them. I got better tax loopholes than charity."

"I...I thought..."

"Thanks for trying to think. Just do what I hired you to do. Get that camp. My attorneys are coming tomorrow to discuss possible lawsuits. If I have to use that option, you will not receive a paycheck for being useless."

The old hag is sealing Lana's conviction. She throws her arms in the air. "I'm a purchaser! I purchase property that's FOR SALE. I'm not a coercer, and I'm also NOT a construction foreman! I...I..."

Mrs. Badmorn raises her hand to block Lana's face. "Don't say anymore. I'm sorry." Her brows lift in an exaggerated mournful expression. "It was a threat. I need your help, and I put aside enough funding to give you a very comfortable living the rest of your life...IF you stick with me."

Lana rubs her neck, closes her eyes, and nods. It's not the right time.

"Now, dear, help me to the car. Where the hell is Silas anyways? Where is the limo?"

"There was a glitch. His plan to scare everyone off backfired. The police got him."

Beverly Badmorn sighs loudly, reminding Lana of a snake hissing. "Great. Now we have to bale his assss out."

"And get the limo out of impound."

"Tsk, we just got it back from the repair shop yesterday." Beverly plops herself into Lana's Lexis. "What a dumbass."

Lana closes the passenger door for Mrs. Badmorn and walks to the driver's side. She tosses her bag to the back seat.

Mrs. Badmorn is tapping on her cellphone. "I'm calling my lead attorney. I'm tired of playing games."

19

IT'S GONNA BE DANTASTIC

Senior sits at his desk, where he has been all night. With the latest episode from Badmorn in her efforts to take Sedation Falls, he worries for the safety of his campers, let alone one of them having a heart attack because of her antics. Walter saw the police pick up Silas, but it doesn't mean he won't do it again. Senior wonders what else she could have up her sleeve. A heavy knot twisting in his gut tells him all this is coming to a head. He rented a tour bus this morning. It took most of his emergency fund to do it, but this is an emergency. He needs everyone out so he can meet the witch mono a mono. The rest of the group can go on a very pleasant field trip.

Walter strolls into the office and smiles—his mustache stroked down like a contented cat. "Hey, Kemosabe, you eat breakfast yet?"

Junior rolls over in his cot and props himself onto one elbow. He rubs his eyes. "Breakfast?"

"Yeah, it's pretty good. French toast day." Walter pushes a knee against Junior's cot to move it out of the way.

Junior jumps out of it wearing striped boxer shorts and folds up the portable bed.

Senior rests his head in his hands. "I'm not hungry."

Junior tosses on a pair of khaki shorts and his Camp Sedation Falls T-shirt. "I am. I'll bring something back for you, Dad."

Senior sighs. "Sounds good."

Walter takes a seat at his desk, opens a drawer, and pours a shot of Jim Beam.

"Now?" Senior asks, weary.

Walter stands, bringing the shot glass along with him to Senior's desk. "It's fer you. You look like you need it."

Senior smiles meekly. "Thanks, you're right." He drinks it down, shivering with the heat of alcohol flowing down his throat.

Walter leans on Senior's desk. "What's up?"

"We need to send the Seniors on a field trip. The hairs on the back of my neck are tingling. Something's brewing."

"Something is alright, Lana told me all about it."

"Lana? When did you see her?"

Walter straightens, and pats down wild mustache hairs. "She was in the woods."

Senior is agog. "In the woods? With Silas?" He stands. "What the hell?"

"Seems they were in cahoots in tryin' to scare us away, an' ol' Silo was gonna shoot me, so she knocked his gun out of his hand. Then, Rizzy sat his ass down. I thanked the lady fer savin' my life, but she said she was savin' a cub. So, we smoked a peace joint."

Walter's shorthand account leaves Senior blinking in confusion.

Walter takes a breath. "Any who, Lana told me Badmorn is hirin' a team of lawyers to sue us fer breakin' the law, so she can take Sedation Falls cheaper than one of Dingo's shirts."

Now, Senior's confusion is turning to outrage. "What laws? We didn't break any laws."

Walter gazes at the ceiling in thought. "Hm, she said we put our campers at dire risk." He counts on his fingers. "Mildred got locked in the toilet, we put old folks on peddle boats with no life vests...uh, unsupervised drinkin, and four, dangerous swimmin' pool games. I think there was a fifth thing, but I forget." His eyes grow wide, making his bushy brows do a sit-up. "Oh yeah! We hog-tied and beat up Silas."

Senior's eyes bulge. He can almost feel steam escaping through his nose. "What? That's ridiculous! I'm surprised you're not pissed off about this."

Walter strolls to his desk, sits, opens a drawer, places another shot glass on the desk, and pours himself a shot of Jim Beam. "Well, ol' friend, with my future attorney granddaughter, Samantha, and Lana on our side, I think ol' hag, Badmorn has screwed the pooch tryin' to mess with us."

"You think so?"

"Our little bag lady is fierce. She'll get to the bottom of this. Salute." Walter sucks down his shot and shivers.

Calmer, Senior picks up his glass and walks over to Walter's desk. "So, you like Lana now?"

Walter pours two more shots of Jim Beam. "I never hated her. I rather admired her dedication to the job."

Senior shakes his head and chuckles. "Right, but I feel a showdown at the OK Corral coming soon."

Walter lifts his glass. "Think you can handle it?"

Senior holds up his shot. "Oh yeah."

The men tap glasses and swallow their drinks.

***

Stitch and Junior are performing a head count as campers board the tour bus. Nurse Oyomama is completing med checks.

Harley stops at the door of the bus. "Do we hafta go? Kelly and I can hang back an' watch the place."

Stitch stands askew, hand on his hip. "Do you know where we're goin'?"

Harley shakes his head, no. "I wasn't listenin' to the morning announcements."

Stitch gasps in surprise. "My man, this is one dantastic trip!"

"Dantastic?"

"Yeah, dang fantastic! We are gonna ride an old timey steam train, see a show, ride a chair lift up a mountain, an' dey even got a zoo!" Enthusiasm bursts from Stitch. He seems to be vibrating from excitement. "An' it's only two hours from here."

"And shopping," Bethany calls out from inside the bus.

"What's it called?"

"Tweetsie Railroad."

Harley guffaws at the name. Kelly nudges him. "Let's go. It sounds like fun."

Stitch smiles wide. "Hey, you paid for it when you booked the camp."

Kelly pulls on Harley's arm. "See? Let's go."

"Tell you what…" Harley leans against the open bus door, blocking others from embarking. A few campers begin to grumble behind him. "How 'bout we follow you on the bike? Didn't you say it's only two hours from here?"

Junior and Stitch pause in consideration. Junior shrugs. "Why not?"

"All right! Let's go." Harley and Kelly trot away to the relief of the line. The rest of the campers enter the bus.

Leigh Ann and Chef Fry arrive with coolers filled with sandwiches, water, and juice. People cheer. Leigh smiles vapidly, a half-smile, half-grimace.

Walter approaches, lifts a lid from one of the coolers, and digs around in it. "Any beer in here?"

Leigh Ann sniffs, "Mr. Darling said it's an alcohol free trip."

Walter huffs, "He did, aye?"

Chef Fry loads the last cooler onto the bus. "You work it out with him."

"Are you goin'?"

"Naw man, I gotta stay an' make dinna' for y'all. 'Sides, I got an itch, Mr. Darlin' might be needin' me."

Walter shakes Chef's hand. "I think he'll need ya too." He waves toward the group in the bus. "I'll take care of these ol' fossils."

"Speak for yourself!" Brittany shouts.

Walter gets on the bus and shakes hands with the driver. "Looks like we're ready to go."

The roar of a motorcycle engine tells him Harley is following behind.

***

Richard Darling Senior and Chef Fry stand in the driveway as the bus motors down the lane.

Senior rubs the penknife in his pocket. "You ready?"

"Hell, yeah." Chef Fry winks and smiles.

20

TWEETSIE RAILROAD

"Tweetsie Railroad." Wilson laughs, and pokes Muffy, who's sitting beside him. She giggles. He continues, but talks like an excited little boy. "We're gonna ride da train, wee! Whose idea is this?"

"Mine," Walter booms from a row behind him. "You got somethin' to say 'bout it?"

Wilson straightens in his seat, not turning his head to face Walter. "Uh, no...no, I was just askin'."

Muffy covers her mouth with her hand and snickers.

"Dumbass," Walter mumbles. He's sitting next to his granddaughter, Samantha. Junior is sitting across the aisle from her. The two are chatting it up and seem to be hitting it off. Junior's not a bad kid, but he has to learn things the hard way. Yet, Walter finds that trait to be a rather positive one. *It'll help him learn not to make the same mistake twice; like putting important papers under piles of Publisher's Clearinghouse ads.*

Another of the kid's mistakes was Amy, one of last year's counselors. He jumped for her faster than a cat leaping out of water. Guys tend to feel that way toward the first girl they get naked in front of. Walter was lucky. He married the first girl he bumped uglies with and never regretted it. Amy wasn't good for Junior anyways. She was a loosey goosey. Junior and Samantha? Walter believes he could stand Junior as a grandson-in-law.

A jab in his side jerks Walter from his thoughts.

"I said, isn't this bus nice?" Samantha strokes the leather seats.

"Ten times better than the one we rode last year, isn't it, Mr. Evans?" Junior's eyes are on him.

"Uh, yeah, yeah...it sure is," Walter stammers. "We went all out fer this." He raises his voice. "An' I don't care 'bout the stupid name of the park!"

Wilson chuckles.

Stitch jumps up. "Let's sing camp songs. It makes the trip go faster."

"Let's not. I'm watching *The Young and the Restless.* I love these TVs on the backs of the seats," Bethany shouts.

Stitch acts as though he doesn't hear her and begins, "There was a boy an' a girl inna a little canoe..."

Several voices shout, "Nooo."

Cheerful as ever, Stitch sings, "One-hundred bottles of beer on da wall, one hundred bottles of..."

"Nooo!"

Stitch stops, but only for a few seconds, when a wide grin forms on his face. "I gots it," and he sings; his voice, smooth and mellow. "I've got sunshine...on a cloudy day. When it's cold outside...I got the month of May. Well, I guess you'd say, what could make me feel this way..."

Many voices join in, "My girl."

"Talkin' bout my girl…"

"My girl, Ooooo…" Laughter breaks out on the bus as Stitch and the riders continue their song.

At the gate, Walter pays for the bus and motorcycle behind them. Stitch secures wristbands to the campers and runs to give Harley and Kelly theirs.

As the campers depart the bus, they are surrounded by an old-time Western town complete with a steam train. Junior and Stitch carry the coolers and lead the group to their specified area, a nice pavilion adjacent to what appears to be a fort from the olden days.

"Time to eat?" Will asks, pushing his walker along.

Stitch swaggers up to him, hands in his pockets, and he's chewing on a blade of grass. "Not yet, cow poke. We gots some varmints to take care of first." He inhales the grass and coughs on it.

"Oopsy," Muffy titters.

A park employee arrives pushing a wheelchair. Stitch, still in cowboy mode, presents it to Will. "This horse is fer you."

"Wonderful." Will sits in it. "This is nice."

"She's a beaut all right."

An employee shouts, "Anyone else need one?"

Bethany begins to raise her arm, but Tiffany pulls it down. "Your horse will get in the way. You'll be fine."

Bethany rolls her eyes. "Tsk."

"Good." The employee checks his watch. "We board the Yukon Queen in forty-five."

"Thanks, pardner, we'll be there." Stitch waves.

BANG!

Campers scream in surprise. Mildred throws herself on the ground and covers her head.

"Guys! Look!" Junior points. "They're acting a shoot-out. It's a show."

BANG! BANG! Men in western garb shoot at each other. Women in long dresses pretend to be frightened and scream.

"I can't get up!" It's Mildred this time.

Walter rolls her to her back and tries to lift her to a seated position, but the piercing pain in his back makes him stop. "Sit up, woman!"

Mildred tries, but only rolls around in the dirt. "I can't!"

Junior and Stitch rush over to help. It's an effort. Leigh Ann arrives to finish getting her to her feet by hefting her rear. Leigh Ann sniffs. "Are you okay?"

Mildred nods while brushing dirt from her clothes. "I'm fine."

Bethany elbows Tiffany. "Heh, it was a lot easier to get me up."

Tiffany scowls at Bethany. "That's because I was pumped up on adrenaline. You could lose a few pounds."

"Oh, stop, they say women my age need a few extra pounds. It helps us live longer."

"Yeah, and the ones that have to pick you up die sooner."

"You're not funny, Tif."

"The Yukon Queen. Sounds fun, doesn't it, Love Bug?" Muffy squeezes Wilson's hand.

"Sure does, Sugar Drop," Wilson agrees, guiding her to the train station.

Walter thumbs at the couple. "I'm getting' diabetic jus' listenin' to 'em."

"Oh, Grandpa." Samantha says that a lot. She takes Junior's hand and heads for the train.

Dingo and Miss Pat are holding hands, as well as Harley and Kelly. Bethany holds onto Tiffany's elbow for support, and Stitch is pushing Will in the wheelchair.

Walter gazes down at his hands. "I haven't held someone's hand since Helen passed away six years ago," he says to himself.

"Ahem." Scottish Bob nudges him and holds out a hand. "I'd a be awnaud ta hold ye hand, pawtnah."

Walter tilts his head up to match Bob's eyes. His mustache quivers. "Git the fuck outta here!"

"Ye appeared ta feum a billy."

Walter nods. "You can be my friend, but I sure as hell ain't gonna hold hands."

"Ah, so right, ya we cutty dobber."

"I'm gonna consider that a compliment. At least I don't wear a skirt." Walter trods ahead of Bob.

Bob shakes his head. "A stubby manky tadger fer sure."

Steam bellows from the 1800s style Yukon Queen.

"All aboard!" The engineer calls.

Rapturous buzz pulsates in Walter's chest and he does his best to hide it. He used to have a Lionel model train set in his spare bedroom. It filled the whole room. Helen hated it. She said they couldn't have overnight guests because of his damn hobby. He thought it was a good way to keep company at bay. He had that set since he was a kid, but Helen's wishes won out when she got sick—sold it at a damn garage sale for fifty bucks. He loved that set not so much for its value, but because it brought back the memory of his father taking the family on the steam train to Washington, DC. It was the best day of his life.

Walter takes a seat on a bench near the front of the passenger car. Who should plop herself right next to him? Ostrich-eyed Bethany. He leans away from her. "Shouldn't ya be sittin' with yer girlfriend?"

"Ha," Bethany says, but she's not laughing, she's frowning. "She's not my friend. When I sat next to her, she told me to act like a tree and leaf."

"Leaf?"

She leans in toward Walter and says it loud enough for the whole train to hear, "Leave!"

Walter winces, holding a finger to his ear. "Woman, I'm right here!"

"Sorry about that. I'm upset. I have so much trouble making friends. What's wrong with me?"

Nothin', 'cept bein' nosey, bossy, and puttin' yer bug eyes into everyone's business. He shrugs. "Dunno."

"You're my only friend."

Walter has a hand on the seat between himself and Bethany, so she won't scoot any closer. Instead, she places her hand on his. He moves it away to pet his mustache. "Listen. You can sit there if'n ya don't blather on at me 'bout nothin'."

"What's nothing?"

"Everythin'. Jus' be quiet an' let me enjoy the ride."

Bethany blinks, the corners of her mouth droop, and she nods slowly.

"Thanks."

Bethany sighs loud and long. "That's what friends are for."

Walter's mustache curls up. "Great."

TOOT! TOOT! The train is finally moving. Walter is soothed by the clickety clack of the wheels going over the track. He sits beside a window and gazes at the scenery passing by. The train crosses an old wooden bridge. He is in 1950 all over again. He can almost feel his father's breath at the back of his head to catch a glimpse of the towns they pass through. *Wait a minute.*

Walter turns and faces a huge set of eyeballs. He glares at them.

"What? I want to look too," Bethany defends.

"Ain't there an empty bench back there you can sit at?"

"I'll look like a loser sitting by myself."

Walter shakes his head and sighs when the train comes to a screeching stop.

A woman near the back, dressed in period costume, stands and shouts, "It's those bandits!"

The scene outside the window is a replica of an old west town. Two men in bandanas holding fake guns announce they are going to hold up the train. A guy wearing a badge and his deputy step out of the jail and confront the two. They all monkey around like the three stooges, only it's four of them. Then, they have a shootout.

Bethany claps her hands. "Isn't this fun?"

Walter gripes, "Ain't they done yet?"

The train finally moves on after the sheriff wins with a *cha...cha...cha*. Relief.

"You're such a curmudgeon." Bethany leans back to her proper spot on the bench.

"Curmudgeon? Where you learn a word like that?"

Her bottom jaw juts forward. "From knowing you!" Bethany crosses her arms.

"Hmph." That fake hold-up replaced the memory of Walter's father to the one of Silas taking aim at him in the woods and it pisses him off. After ten minutes of blessed silence from Bethany, the train stops again. "What in Sam hell? Another stupid show?"

Bethany stands. "No, fool, the ride is over."

This pisses him off even more. He throws up his arms. "Well, that was fuckin' lame."

"Walter, your language."

"Walter, your language," Walter mimics with a high voice.

Bethany huffs, "I can't believe you." And makes her way down the aisle to depart the train.

Walter notices Tiffany pushing Will on the wheelchair. "Where's Stitch?"

Tiffany stops to answer, "Oh, he's helping the other campers. It's no problem. I'll take care of him."

"Thanks doll," Will calls over a shoulder.

She mouths, *He's loaded*, and rubs her fingers together to indicate money.

This eases Walter's mood.

***

A black Lexus drives up the lane toward what was once Caring Souls Adult Center, but now is a pile of metal and wood. The car is parked, and Lana steps out. Things have slipped beyond her control, and she doesn't like it one bit. Mrs. Badmorn has become more irrational by the day. She seemed pleased when the home burned down, and it was conveniently empty. There was an investigator here, but Badmorn has them in her pockets. Lana used to be in control of situations and has no idea when it flipped. "I'm sure they missed something." Lana pulls her hair up and slips on a pair of work gloves. *I need to find it today. They will finish this up tomorrow.* She scurries to the stack of metal and begins pulling out pieces of bent siding and copper piping. She runs her hands over every piece. *If lightning really hit it, I should find burn streaks, or a hole where it entered.*

***

After a delicious lunch of ham and Swiss sandwiches made by Chef Fry, the group stops at Diamond Lil's for a Can-Can girl show. The dancers' bloomers are brimming with ruffles and cover too much for Walter's liking.

Harley nudges Walter. "Pretty lame, huh?"

"An' they don't even sell beer here."

Stitch, however, has enough enthusiasm for the whole camp as the girls pull him up on stage and the kid struts his stuff with the best of them. He kicks those skinny-ass legs high in the air.

Stepping out of the fake Saloon, Walter is hit with the combination of heat and high humidity. Worse than that, children are running amok everywhere—their faces smeared with the remains of melted chocolate ice cream. "I never liked children. Not counting Samantha, of course. She was nothing like these feral creatures."

A youngster cuts in front of him almost tripping him. "Hey!" Walter's mustache flutters as though reaching to snatch the child.

Junior strolls up to him, and he's still holding Samantha's hand. *Too damn hot fer that. Sweaty palms...rank.*

"Hot day, huh?" Junior asks. *Dumb question.* He continues, "Let's take the campers on the chair lift up the mountain. We should get a cool breeze up there."

"It'll be fun." Samantha smiles. That smile melts Walter every time, no matter how cranky he is.

It'll get him away from these little gremlins, but some of the campers want to shop first. Walter finds a place in the shade to sit and wait. A boy, looking to be around seven or eight, stops his running to stare at him. Walter stares back.

The kid pats his own eyebrows. "Are those real?"

Walter instinctively pets his brows. "Yeah."

The youth points. "Is that a squirrel tail under your nose?"

Annoyed. "H...heck, no, son. This is my mustache." Walter pats it down.

"You got more hair on your face than my daddy gots on his head."

"I'm sure your daddy would like to hear that." *Little son-of-a...*

"There you are." The apparent daddy of the urchin arrives and takes the kid's hand. His attention turns to Walter. "I'm sorry if my son was bothering you."

Walter observes the hair on Daddy's head. Looks pretty healthy and thick to him. *Dumb kid.* "No problem. Glad you found him."

"Whew, you got that right. There are so many children here, he was blending right in. I better get him back to the wife." Daddy kneels in front of his son, and that's when Walter sees it. The man has a bald spot the size of a saucer on the back of his noggin. "You really scared your mother and me."

The child lowers his head. "I'm sorry."

It didn't sound sincere to Walter.

The father stands and waves to him while hand in hand with his son, moves on. Walter closes his eyes to enjoy a slight cooling breeze but instead, it seems to be getting hotter, even in the shade of the tree.

"Mr. Evans, look!"

Walter's eyes open to Stitch standing in front of him in cowboy boots and a Stetson hat.

"I'm a cowboy!" Stitch places his thumbs into the front pockets of his khaki shorts and does a jig, his lanky legs swimming in those boots. He has no definition at all in his calves, and his eyes barely clear the brim of that hat. Stitch sings and dances, and it is drawing a crowd. "Ridin', ridin' along. Oh, a cowboy needs a horse, needs a horse, needs a horse. And a cowboy needs a hat, needs a hat, needs a hat. An' fancy boots if he wants to keep ridin' along, ridin', ridin' along."

When he is finished, Stitch removes his hat and bows. Folks drop money into it.

"That's how it's done, son!" Walter claps. His mood boosted, he joins the other campers to wait for the lift. It is a ski lift with benches hanging over the landscape with room on each for only two people. Walter thumbs at it. "You actually believe we can all git on that thing?"

"Stitch and I will help you." Junior smiles, puffing out his chest.

Walter eyes Stitch, who weighs maybe 120 pounds. "Yer gonna need more than that."

Junior is confident. "They said they'll slow it down for us and the girls will help too."

Samantha raises her arm and lifts up one of Leigh Ann's.

Walter's brows arch like two grey hissing cats. "I don't know 'bout that."

And...it's on. Most of the campers get on the lift with little trouble. Harley steps in to help Will onto one and Scottish Bob sits with him. Walter's turn. He stands in his spot, eyes squinched shut. The seat gently pushes into his knees, causing him to sit, and up he goes.

"See? That wasn't so bad."

Walter's eyes pop open. He glares at the person next to him...Bethany.

"How'd you git on?"

"Same way you did, you old coot."

"Everywhere I look, there you are. Like a wet hair. I can't shake you off."

"You know you like me."

"Fake news."

Bethany frowns and falls back against the bench, causing it to swing.

Walter grabs the bar in front of him. "Woman, don't do that!"

Bethany throws up her arms. "Whatever."

As Walter's heart rate returns to running speed, he notices the chair in front of them. It's Wilson and Muffy and they're making out. He waves in their direction. "Lookit that. Ungodly behavior, an' they're not payin' no attention to the scenery."

Bethany pokes him. "It's romantic. Did you ever go to the drive-in with a girl and miss the whole movie?"

Walter's stomach churns. "If I'm payin' to see a movie, I'm gonna see the movie. Romantic my hairy butt cheeks." He chuffs. "Lookit that PDA."

"PDA?" Bethany nods. "Oh, yes, public display of affection."

"No. Public display of ass. He looks like an ass to me."

Rumbling of thunder. The sun is now covered by dark foreboding clouds.

Bethany looks up. "Oh no, we're only halfway through the ride. Do you think it'll hold off until we're done?"

"No."

A flash of lightning makes her jump, causing the bench to swing again.

"Dag nab it, woman." Walter's grip on the bar is white knuckled.

***

Back at the camp, Richard Darling Senior's concerns come to fruition. Sure enough, a black limo rolls up the lane. He and Chef Fry step out to meet Mrs. Badmorn. The limo stops, Silas exits and opens the rear passenger door.

Senior isn't sure how to greet the woman stepping out, so he only nods to her.

She glares at him, mouth set firm.

"Hello, Mrs. Badmorn." Senior waves toward Silas. "I thought he was arrested."

"You never heard of bail?" The corner of her mouth curls into a sneer. "Besides, he was unarmed, thanks to you."

"I want my gun back," Silas demands.

Senior smiles, but he's sure it appears stiff and mocking as if holding in a laugh. "I'm sorry, but Walter threw it in Lake Watchawanna." He coughs to hold back a gufall.

Silas growls, hands balled into fists.

Mrs. Badmorn places her palm on Silas's arm. "I'll buy you a shiny new one." She turns to Senior. "We need to talk."

"That's fine. We'll go to my office. But without your strongman there."

"I could use some help in the kitchen," Chef Fry says.

Mrs. Badmorn nods to Silas to go. His shoulders drop and he sighs—a kid forced to walk to school.

Chef and Silas move on to the kitchen while Senior and Mrs. Badmorn take a seat in his office. She's holding a large manilla envelope, opens it, and brings out a stack of papers.

She takes a deep breath. "As you may know by now, I have withdrawn any monetary offers to your camp. I have something much more lucrative...to me."

"Where is Lana? I thought she is your representative." Senior was hoping she would be here.

Mrs. Badmorn's eyes narrow. "I no longer need her service. This will be in the hands of my attorneys after I show you this."

Senior stands. He was warned she's going to try to force the camp away from him.

"Show us what? How stupid you are?" Dingo is standing in the office doorway.

Senior doesn't want Dingo involved. He means well, but the man is good at screwing things up.

Mrs. Badmorn holds up her papers. "Excuse me? I have proof how stupid you are. All I have to do is snap my fingers, and I can have Silas really shove your head up your ass, because according to my information, it's already been there."

"Oh yeah?" Two buttons pop off of Dingo's shirt.

Senior needs to bring things down a notch. "Okay, okay, that's enough."

Dingo enters the room, giving Mrs. Badmorn the evil eye on his way to Walter's desk. "I'm part owner. I need to be here and see what this witch is gonna do next."

Senior sighs, "You gave us part of the down payment, and spent much more than that."

Dingo nods, continuing his glare. "Uh, huh, part owner."

Senior scratches his head. He must continue to speak to Badmorn in spite of Dingo. "We know all about your plan to prove we need to be shut down because of the treatment to our campers, but it won't work. Our campers love this place, they'll never witness against us."

She lifts a finger. "Al contraire, I don't need witnesses."

***

Lana pulls out several planks of charred wood. She can't find any evidence of gas fumes, or remains of something purposely set afire. A lightning bolt would leave black streaks where the bolt traveled. There has been no sign of that. She returns to the metal scraps. The gloves protect her hands from the sharp edges as she examines each piece. The sky darkens. A rumble of thunder. Lana opens the flashlight app on her phone, and that's when she spots it, a black hole with an explosive pattern surrounding it over what appears to be the cover of an electrical panel.

***

Large drops of rain fall on Walter's head, followed quickly by a downpour. Bright lightning flashes high above.

"Christ on a cracker. Didn't Junior check the damn weather?"

"It's a pop-up storm."

BOOM! Crash of thunder. Bethany screams, "We gotta get off of this."

FLASH-BOOM! Lightning hits Wilson. Next to him, Muffy screams.

"Oh my God!" Bethany jumps, the lift sways wildly.

Walter braces himself to the point of every muscle throbbing.

Smoke drifts from the top of Wilson's head before he slumps onto Muffy's lap. She continues her screaming. The operator stops the ride as EMTs arrive to remove Wilson and Muffy.

"This is horrible," Bethany shouts.

"Dang, worst field trip ever!" shouts Harley from a lift behind them.

Walter doesn't answer. He's still frozen in place. The ride operator must peel his fingers from the bar.

***

"You never dealt with a millionaire before, have you?" Mrs. Badmorn scoffs. "I get what I want. I tried to be nice, but..."

"When the hell have you ever been nice? Ha!" Dingo pulls his shirt together.

Senior rubs his forehead. "Dingo. Please?"

Mrs. Badmorn continues as if not hearing him. "You've broken the law." She glares over her papers. "Many times, from what I'm seeing here. All I have to do is make one phone call, and you all go to jail. The camp will go into receivership, and then it will be mine...or you can sign it over to me now, and your reputation will stay intact."

Dingo slams his hands on the desk. "Now, why would we want to do that?"

Mrs. Badmorn considers Dingo as though watching a man drowning next to a raft. "You won't go to jail, and you'll be able to buy a camp somewhere else."

"Can I see those?" Senior holds out a hand. Mrs. Badmorn gives him the papers. He studies them. The way she wrote up the offenses makes Camp Sedation Falls more like Camp Senseless Falls. It sounds so bad, he wouldn't send his ex-wife there, and he can't stand her.

He passes the stack to Dingo. After a minute of reading— "This is nuts!"

Senior's heart sinks to the pit of his stomach. "It's worded really bad, but it's all true."

Dingo drops the papers onto Senior's desk and rubs his hands through his messy hair. "Shit."

***

The tour bus full of Camp Sedation Falls campers pulls into the parking lot of the Caldwell Memorial Hospital. Once parked, everyone rushes to the doors at once, causing a jam. Walter stands and shouts, "Listen up! We all can't go in there. Junior an' I will go. This bus is a lot more comfortable than the damn waiting room. I'll have Junior call Sammy to let y'all know if Wilson and Muffy died."

An audible gasp from the passengers.

"Grandpa." Samantha is shaking her head. "Let us know how they are...dead or not!"

Walter winks. "Right, right, right." He and Junior leave the bus and enter the hospital through the emergency doors.

Junior arrives at the nurses' station before Walter. "We're here for Wilson Ball and Muffy Morrow," Junior pants.

The nurse gazes at a computer screen. "Yes, they're in rooms 1-A and B. Completely shocking what happened to them. Get it? Shocking?"

"What's wrong with you woman? Our friends could be dead!" Walter's mustache shudders like a buzzard quivering its feathers.

She smacks her head. "Oh, I'm sorry, you haven't heard. You can go on back there." The nurse points behind her.

"Wow, what's wrong with people?" Junior asks Walter.

They arrive at room 1 and open the door. There are four sections separated by drawn curtains around the beds. Junior points at the letter A on the wall beside one.

Walter pulls open a curtain expecting the worst. He envisions Wilson's face covered with a sheet. Dead.

Instead, Wilson is sitting on the side of the bed wrapped in a gown. He smells of burnt hair, but the wild brush on his head is still intact. The fuzz on his arms and legs is gone and a red streak runs along his right arm. "Hi guys." He waves.

"Wilson, you're alive!" Junior rushes to hug him.

"Yeah, whew, scary moment there. Fried my clothes clean off, and look." Wilson strokes his arm. "No hair. No pubes either, wanna see?" He begins to pull the cloth of his gown aside.

"No!" Walter holds out a hand in a stop motion. "We'll believe you."

"Except for this sore spot on my arm, I feel great." Wilson leans forward and whispers, "How is Muffy? I don't hear anything over there. Man, she better be okay."

The emergency doctor enters their area. "Believe it or not, he's free to go. Amazing. We want to keep him overnight for observation, but he refuses. Other than the slight burn and elevated heart rate, he's fine." A nurse enters to check Wilson's blood pressure and heart rate. She shows the results to the doctor. He raises his brows in surprise. "Wow, looks like everything's back to normal." He pats Wilson on his thigh. "You must have a guardian angel."

Wilson grins wide. "I do. Her name is Muffy. How is she, doc?"

The doctor smiles. "We'll have her tell you." He turns to his nurse. "Is she dressed yet?" The nurse nods. "You can see her now."

Wilson wraps the gown around himself and jumps off of the bed. He pulls open the curtain to bed B. Muffy stands before him. She's wearing a sling over her left shoulder. A bandage is wrapped around her hand, wrist, and arm up to her elbow.

She smiles sweetly. "Hey."

"We believe the bolt traveled through Mr. Ball into Miss Morrow through the elbow. It then traveled out through her hand. She has second-degree burns on her hand and wrist." The doctor jots on a clipboard. "I sent in a prescription for her. The dressing needs changed at least once a day, and she can take Ibuprofen for pain."

Muffy nods to him. "Thank you."

"I'd like to see you again in two weeks."

"You got it."

Back on the bus, everyone cheers when they see Muffy and Wilson. He regales them with his harrowing story—how the zipper of his pants liquified, and thanked God it didn't melt onto his family jewels, and how hairless he is down there.

Walter instructs the bus driver to stop at an ABC store on their way back to camp. "I need three bottles of Jack after today."

***

Senior picks up the pen to sign the papers. His heart aches. Everything he's done, this whole place has become a part of him, only to give it all up by signing his name. He wipes a tear away with a finger when suddenly, his breath is caught in his chest, and he gasps. He takes his lucky penknife from a front pocket, and rubs it with his eyes closed, wishing for some kind of magic solution. *If only I could open my eyes and she would be gone.*

"I can't wait for you all day." Mrs. Badmorn taps a finger on her empty envelope.

Dingo snatches the papers from Senior's desk. "You know what?" He turns toward Mrs. Badmorn. "You can shove these right up your..."

"Stop!" Lana barges through the door. "Don't sign anything."

21

GOODBYE TO BAD RUBBISH

Lana's soaked to the skin and holds a large army-green sheet of metal. She thrusts it out in front of her. "Look!" She points at a black hole surrounded by what looks like a Rorschach test to Senior. She continues, "This was the cover of the electrical panel...and look at this." She opens her fist to reveal four bullet casings. "I found them where the panel used to be. I can't believe they were missed by the fire inspector."

"Caring Souls was at the border of hunting grounds," Mrs. Badmorn rebuts.

Senior walks over to Lana. "Hunting is outlawed in this area." His hand touches hers as she pours the shells into his palm. Her glance is nothing like one of a stone cold purchaser. She really cares. He studies the casings. "These are incendiary rounds."

"They exploded the panel similar to a lightning strike," Lana asserts. "Only this is a circular pattern. A lightning strike would have longer streaks moving away from the initial impact."

Senior has never seen such emotion from her. It's sexy...although the wet shirt sticking to her breasts helps too.

"Silas!" Mrs. Badmorn stands, dropping the envelope.

Silas and Chef Fry enter the office chuckling. Silas is patting Chef on the back. "I'm lookin' forward to trying that on my grill. Never tasted ribs so tender."

The two stop at the scene in front of them.

Mrs. Badmorn points at Senior and Lana. "Finish them!"

Silas shrugs with palms facing up in confusion. "What?"

"They know what you did, finish them off." Badmorns' hair is unraveling from its updo. Strands fall in front of her face. She pulls a small pistol from her purse and presents the butt of the gun to her henchman.

Silas steps slowly toward her pointing at himself. "What I did? I was merely doing your bidding. It was easier to burn it down than remodel the whole damn place. Not to mention the hefty insurance money that came along with it. And did I get any of that?" His face is inches from hers. "NO!"

Lana joins him, dripping rainwater onto Mrs. Badmorn's lap. "You pushed us too far. We've had enough."

Mrs. Badmorn huffs, turns the pistol around, and now it's pointing at Lana and Silas. They step back. Badmorn brushes water from her lap with her free hand and straightens. "All of you will rot in prison."

Senior nudges Lana and Silas aside to face her. "So will you." His anger has blinded him to the fact she is holding a gun.

All glare at one another. It's a stand-off.

Mrs. Badmorn's eyes narrow. "You're all not worth it." She hands Silas the pistol and he pockets it.

The tour bus parks in front of the dining hall. The campers pile out, walking quickly through the rain, and pour into the dining hall, laughing and talking.

"Where the hell is everybody?" Walter pushes the office door open and stares at the group inside. Several campers gather behind him, including Wilson, who's still wearing a hospital gown and bracelet.

Senior breaks and approaches Wilson. "What happened?"

"I got hit by lightnin'." Wilson has a goofy smile planted on his face.

"Another law broken. You injured a Senior Citizen in your care," Mrs. Badmorn calls out behind Senior.

"I got an alert for you," Dingo shouts at her. "Arson is mandatory prison time." He shakes the stack of papers in her face. "All your money won't get you out of it." He tosses them into the trash can next to Walter's desk.

Walter storms into the room. "What in Samhill is goin' on?"

"Shoot-out at the OK corral." Chef Fry chuckles.

Lana places the panel onto Walter's desk. "And no one is winning." She wraps her arms around herself and shivers.

Senior pulls the blanket from Junior's cot tucked in the corner of the room and drapes it around Lana. He lingers with his arms enfolding her and whispers, "Thank you."

She responds in a low voice, "Don't thank me yet."

Walter saunters to the door and calls into the dining room, "Samantha, we need an intermediary." He turns, strolls to his desk, pulls out a notebook, pen, a bottle of Jim Beam, and a stack of paper cups.

Samantha enters and picks up the notebook and pen.

Campers crowd at the open office door. Bethany pushes to the front. "We'll be your jury."

The others nod and verbalize agreement.

Walter waves to Silas and Lana. He is in full attorney mode. If he messes up, he figures Sammy will help him. "Please be seated."

Senior pulls open Junior's cot so that everyone can sit.

"Ladies and gentlemen. We are here to determine if we should call the cops, and on whom?" Walter raises a finger in the air dramatically. "OR. Should we all call a truce and go our separate ways? That is the question."

"I ain't goin' to jail." Silas stabs a finger toward Badmorn. "She made me do it. Hell, I already served five years...ain't gonna serve no more."

Walter nods toward him, and calmly asks, "And how did she make you? Did she hold a gun to your head?"

"No, but..."

"The butt of the matter is, you did what she asked. Why?"

"She paid me to do it. I can't get a real job with my record." Sweat beads on Silas's brow.

"Ah." Walter nods knowingly. "Lana. Were all of your purchases for clients considered...legal?"

Lana licks her lips. "Mostly."

"Ah." Walter nods again. "Did Mrs. Badmorn here pay you to complete," He makes quote marks with his fingers, "*Mostly legal* purchases?"

She nods, then sucks in a breath, "But, I quit when she went too far. I'm not for killing bears or burning down property."

Walter gasps, losing his cool attitude. "Killing bears? What the hell do you mean, killing bears?" He leans over Lana, startling her.

Lana points at Mrs. Badmorn. "She...she was mad Silas didn't kill the bears when he had the chance. That's why he wrecked the limo."

"It's true," Silas chirps.

Walter makes a stirring motion with his hand. His caterpillar brows writhe in anger. "This puts a whole new spin on things."

Senior decides he better step in. Samantha is furiously writing in the notebook. He spreads out his arms. "Okay, okay, let's get it together. We need to be civilized about this."

"No, we don't," Harley shouts from the dining room. "Burn the witch at a stake!"

The others cheer.

Senior places his hands on his hips. "Come on, now. Cut it out."

"Look!" Muffy holds up her burnt arm. "Lightning hit it when I touched Love Bug's willy." She points at Mrs. Badmorn. "She cursed us. She's a witch!"

The crowd cheers, "Burn her!"

"Excuse me? I didn't curse anyone. You are all a bunch of demented fools."

Muffy points. "You're wearing black in the middle of summer."

"Yes, so?"

"A witch!" Harley shouts.

Chef Fry blocks the door. "Y'all calm the fuck down!"

Walter bellows, "Ain't nobody burnin' nobody."

Silas glares at Mrs. Badmorn. "Sounds like a good idea to me."

"In your dreams," Mrs. Badmorn shoots back. She stands. "Maybe I am a witch, and you're all cursed if I don't get this camp." She swings out her arm as though throwing a lightning bolt. Wilson covers his jewels with both hands. There is a collective gasp, and everyone chatters animatedly.

Walter balls his fists. His brows head butt each other in battle. "Dag nab it, woman!"

Mrs. Badmorn smirks and chuckles.

Senior shouts, "She is not a witch. A bitch maybe, but she can't throw spells." He has both arms in the air. "Everyone, please calm down."

Samantha stands, holding her notebook in the air. "I have it!" Everyone quiets to listen to her. "Both of you have broken laws. Mr. Darling probably wouldn't go to jail, but he would face a ton of fines resulting in bankruptcy. Mrs. Badmorn, contracting arson and using strong arm tactics to obtain property are not only pun-ishable by fines, but also mandatory jail time. You can both threaten and report on each other, but both of you will lose."

Silas points at himself. "What about us?"

"You were both accomplices, jail time."

"Fuck."

Lana closes her eyes and sighs heavily.

Walter and his burly brows point at Silas. "You tried to kill me and the bears. Thank Christ Lana stopped you."

Silas scoffs, clicking his tongue. "I wasn't gonna kill no one...shit."

"Since you two failed so miserably, don't expect a paycheck." Mrs. Badmorn pins her hair back, crosses her legs, and straightens her black dress.

Everyone stares incredulously at her. She glances up, no emotion in her eyes. "Beg your pardon?"

Samantha holds her open notebook toward Mrs. Badmorn. "Do you understand what kind of trouble you could be in?"

Mrs. Badmorn rolls her eyes. "Please, that stuff only happens to you people."

Samantha's eyes widen, mouth agape.

Walter has never seen his granddaughter like this before. She's about to explode. His heart fills with pride.

Samantha jabs at her notebook repeatedly with her index finger. "Mandatory! Mandatory jail time. That means, you go to jail no matter how much money you have. There is no spa in confinement."

Mrs. Badmorn leans back in her chair. She licks her lips. The wall of confidence is beginning to crumble. "I need a glass of water."

Walter leans forward against his desk. "Ask fer it politely."

"Tsk, may I have a glass of water?"

Nurse Oyomama is quick to hand her a bottle of water. As Mrs. Badmorn swallows from it, the nurse feels the widow's pulse. "Tis a bit too high."

Mrs. Badmorn pulls her arm away. "I'm fine."

Bethany squeezes through the crowd at the door. "How are you going to fix this mess?"

Tiffany shows beside her. "Maybe we should go home?"

"Hell, no!" A shout from the back. It is Harley. "This is too much fun to watch. I still say, burn the witch."

"I have an idea." Samantha stands on the cot, feet spread wide for balance. She reads from her notebook. "Mrs. Badmorn, if you don't turn in Mr. Darling and shut down Sedation Falls, we won't tell the authorities about what you arranged."

Mrs. Badmorn huffs and switches her crossed legs.

Samantha continues, "Silas and Lana, if you quit working for Mrs. Badmorn, we won't report you."

Silas smiles crookedly. "Easy, no problem. Consider it done."

"I want my woods back." Walter stomps. His eyebrows wobble from the impact.

"They were always your woods. I lied." Lana sighs. "I knew Mr. Darling and Mr. White had no idea how to decipher the mortgage contract."

Senior is wide-eyed. "What about the road?"

Walter could slap himself for not insisting on looking at the contract before agreeing to be a partner. Those damn lawyers use all kinds of confounding language.

Lana bows her head. "The road is legit. That is under the Badmorn estate."

"Damn it."

Mrs. Badmorn stands and pats down her mid-calf dress. "I offered two million a while ago and you rejected it." She focuses her eyes on Senior. "How about two and a half?"

Senior chuffs. His cheeks blow out as though restraining from outright laughter.

Walter will bid more if Senior accepts her offer. It'll take everything he has, but it would be worth it to keep her grubby hands off of the place.

A tense few moments of silence. Mrs. Badmorn is steady, jaw set firm. "Fine...three million, and that's my final offer."

Senior coughs, holding his throat. Nurse Oyomama hands him a bottle of water, and he chugs it down.

Dingo claps his hands. "Great! One mil for me, one for you, an' one for Walter, even though he hasn't been a partner that long."

Walter's hands shake, restrained anger beginning to erupt. "It's not fer sale," he booms. "Right, Kemosabe?"

Senior shrugs, eyes watering from almost choking. "Well...I don't know...I mean, three million? Really?"

Mrs. Badmorn nods. "That's the legal way to take this dump."

People at the door voice disagreement. Stitch shakes his fist at her. "This ain't no dump. You're insultin' my home, you hoaryvatious hag."

"Dang, Tyrone is usin' big words. You in serious trouble, lady," Chef Fry shouts.

There is no way Walter can scare up three million dollars. He must think fast. *Hell, I dunno.*

"I have an idea." Lana is cool and collected. She gets up on the cot, nudging Samantha aside. "Both of you can make money from this."

"Oh, really?" Mrs. Badmorn sneers.

"We're listening." Senior pats Walter on the back. Walter takes that pat as *keep your pie hole shut.*

Lana swings her arm toward the group at the door. "How many of you would love a nice massage or pedicure after a long day of activities?"

Everyone raises their hands, including Walter. "The Badmorn Spa Bed and Breakfast would include the camp in their summer packages. Sedation Falls would include spa days in their schedule. Both of you would be paid for your services and there is a nice, paved lane connecting the two. Get me?"

Mrs. Badmorn scrunches her brows together in confusion. "A B and B?"

"Yes." Lana winks at Senior. "It would be very exclusive, much better than the huge Umstead. Older people are much more focused on health and physical fitness these days. I mean, sixty is the new thirty. You two have the ideal situation here."

"But...but what about the three mil?" Dingo's posture slumps, enlarging his already broad gut. Another button pops on his Hawaiian shirt, leaving him with only two to hold it together.

"You know we got camp T-shirts here," Walter mumbles to Dingo.

Dingo whispers, "They run small."

Mrs. Badmorn plants her chin into the palm of her hand. "I don't know if I can stand you as neighbors."

"I don't know if we can stand you, neither," Walter calls out. Senior elbows him.

Mrs. Badmorn strolls toward Walter, stopping inches from his face. His mustache nearly tickling her drawn-on black eyebrows. She narrows them. "What did you say?"

"He said he don't know if..." Harley is hit sharply in the belly by Kelly's elbow.

Lana spreads her arms. "I can be your liaison. Both of you will pay me to co-ordinate it all."

Mrs. Badmorn is still staring up at Walter. He tilts his head and could swear his mustache is flirting with her penciled brows. "You don't want me to sic my bears on ya...do ya?"

She steps back. "The bears. We need to get rid of them."

"Hell, no, we don't. Just stay outta my woods, an' everyone will be fine. I guarantee."

"Hmph." Mrs. Badmorn returns to her chair.

Everyone holds a collective breath. Both Senior and Mrs. Badmorn have brows furrowed in thought. She is first to speak, "I withdraw my offer."

"Poo." Dingo plops onto the cot Lana is standing on and she swings her arms wildly to stay upright. She hops off.

Mrs. Badmorn continues, "I motion to hire Lana and give this...this spa bed and breakfast idea a try. If it doesn't work, I want the option to buy Sedation Falls at market value."

Murmuring among the group. "It could be a trick," Bethany whispers.

Senior raises a finger. "Excuse me, but I need to speak to my partners."

Dingo and Walter approach Senior. Everyone else leans forward to listen in.

"Privately."

The crowd turns their backs to the door while talking animatedly. The three men huddle. Senior waves to Junior and Samantha to join them. Samantha writes furiously in her notebook.

Silas stretches. "I'm outta here before anyone decides to turn me in. I'd rather be a strip bar bouncer anyways." He shuffles through the crowd.

Mrs. Badmorn calls after him, "You can't take the car."

He stops and asks anyone listening, "Does an Uber come out here?"

Bethany shakes her head, *no.*

He sighs loudly.

"I can take you on the bike," Harley volunteers.

"Your bike?" Silas rubs his eyes.

"Yeah, pretty comfy ride if I say so myself." Harley's chest puffs out in pride.

"Shit. I never rode on the back of a motorcycle."

"You can borrow Kelly's helmet. All you gotta do is hold on an' lean into the curves." Harley gestures to Silas to follow him outside.

Silas trods behind.

"I bet your ass will look yummy on the back of a motorcycle," Tiffany says.

Silas holds up his middle finger at her. "Fuck you."

After several more minutes, the debating men break their pow-wow.

Senior speaks first. "Deal."

"But." Walter's two cents. "If it doesn't pay out, you can have the option to buy this place at twenty-five percent over market value."

Mrs. Badmorn raises an arm as if she's at an auction. "Ten percent."

"Fifteen."

She nods to Samantha. "Done, write that down."

"Also." Senior sidles next to Lana. "I move to hire Lana Curtis as liaison."

Mrs. Badmorn nods. "I second that."

Dingo spits in his hand and holds it out for Mrs. Badmorn to shake. "Let's seal the deal."

One side of her lip curls in disgust. She holds her hands under her chin. "Not like that."

Walter nudges Dingo aside. "Wash yer damn hands, man." And holds out a hand toward Mrs. Badmorn. She grasps Walter's fingertips. "Got a deal?" He asks.

"Deal." She glances at Samantha. "Are you writing this down?"

Samantha nods while scribbling. She stops and stretches her cramping hand. "I have it all right here. I'll type it up and have it notarized."

Wilson holds up a hand. "I'm a notary. I even brought my stamp. It's in the cabin. I'll be right back." He runs out.

Awkward silence while everyone waits for Wilson to return.

Junior approaches his father and whispers, "Dad, what if the plan doesn't work? Are we really gonna sell it to her?"

Senior pats his son on the back. "I'm sure it will. We don't need Badmorn, we're doing great without a spa, but we had to come up with something. We don't want a big court battle."

"Do you think he really is a notary?" Bethany asks, "I mean, maybe that lightning strike fried part of his brain?"

"I hope not." Senior paces. He doesn't trust Badmorn any more than he can trust kissing a viper on the mouth.

Samantha is typing on her phone.

Junior approaches her. "Sending a message to your boyfriend?" He sits beside her trying to get a peek at her phone.

Samantha giggles. "No, silly. I have Word on here. I'll have a document all ready for them to sign. Technology...you know?"

Junior blushes. "Oh, yeah, I knew that. Why didn't you type it up in the first place?"

"Rough draft. Besides, grandpa told me to write it in the notebook, so that's what I did."

"Always good to have a copy." Junior squints one eye. "Sooo…you got a boyfriend?"

Samantha's smile sneaks into a curl on her lips. She winks at Junior. "Maybe, if he gets the clue."

He points at himself, agog.

She grins slyly, and nods.

Nothing matters in the world to Junior right now except for gazing at her smile. He leans over to kiss her.

***

"He's here!" Bethany shouts.

Wilson staggers into the office out of breath, the stamp at ready. He has clothes on now as well. A relief to Walter. He didn't want to look at the man's hairy ass all day.

Samantha's smile turns into a frown of sympathy. "Oh, Mr. Ball, I'm sorry. The online form doesn't need a stamp, just your signature."

Wilson pants to catch his breath. "That's okay, I had to…pant…get dressed anyhow."

She holds out her phone horizontally for Mrs. Badmorn, Senior, Dingo, and Walter to sign. Then, Junior and Lana as witnesses, and last, but not least, Wilson.

There is a collective sigh of relief from everyone.

Mrs. Badmorn moves toward the door as the campers step aside for her. She stops. "I can't drive, and I fired my driver." She addresses the group. "I need a driver."

Lana raises her hand, "I can do it until you find someone."

"Fine, uh, thank you." She struts out toward the limo.

Lana turns to the group on her way out and winks, "Keep your friends close, and your enemies closer."

22

This chapter is intentionally left blank so that you can go to the bathroom, let the dog out, catch your breath from laughing, or whatever. Go ahead, we can wait.

23

SEX ON THE BEACH

Senior sits at his desk and leans on his elbows. He scratches his head. "I guess we gotta put the pickleball court someplace else."

"All that matters is I got my woods back." Walter picks up his backpack holding his pot, cigars, and Jim Beam for a relaxing afternoon. The day before was about all he could take, having to deal with ol' witch, Badmorn. They almost lost the camp until his granddaughter saved the day. "An' here we still had my woods after all. Guess we need to have Samantha go over contracts from here on out." Walter begins to saunter for the office door, when Senior blocks his way.

"What are the activities for today?"

Walter scoffs. "I don't give a shit. Hell, it's a nice day. Let them decide." He moves Senior with one arm. "Now, step aside, Kemosabe, an' don't bother me fer a few hours. It's me time."

Senior's chin quivers like he's about to cry. "What about my me time?"

Walter rolls his eyes. "Oh, for cryin' out loud." He plops his backpack onto his desk, removes a baggy of pot and rolling papers from it and rolls a joint. "Here." He hands it to Senior. "Go somewheres private to smoke it. It'll take the edge off."

"Can I go with you?"

"No, I said it's me time."

"Right, right." Senior takes a whiff of his joint and moves for Walter.

Walter collects his things and moves out. He waves to Senior. "Later."

Walter closes his eyes and breathes in the fresh forest air while taking a seat in a rocking chair. His chapel is how he left it, except for a few vines wrapping on a bench. There is only a little longer than a week of camp left, and the breeze already has a cool crispness to it. The leaves rustle a soothing melody. He lights a joint and takes a deep inhale of the smoke. After holding it in for a few seconds, he releases it from his lungs with a sigh. He begins to doze off.

Something wet and rough is rubbing his bare hairy legs. Walter jerks awake. A bear cub is licking him. He doesn't move, afraid if he tries to shoo the cub away it will anger Rizzy. *Rizzy, where is she?* Walter scans the edges of the clearing and finds her fast asleep in the tall grass. The other cub is dozing under her front paw. The cub in front of him continues licking his leg. He swipes an arm toward it, and whispers, "Shoo, shoo." The cub paws at him. It's already growing sharp claws and it scratches him. "Shit."

The cub stops and stares at him. "Ma!"

Walter waves. "Shh, shh, go see yer ma."

"Ma!"

Rizzy stirs. She blinks several times before lifting her head. The cub next to her awakes and runs toward Walter.

"Christ on a cracker, now what?"

The two cubs wrestle at Walter's feet. Rizzy rises to her four legs and shambles toward him. She growls.

Walter lifts a finger, shaking it at her. "Now listen here, missy. I am an innocent bystander."

She swipes a huge paw, striking the brawling cubs.

"Ma!" one cries, before settling down. Both cubs move on to nibbling flowers.

Rizzy sits on her haunches in front of Walter.

"Miss me?" He can tell by her calm demeanor, she means no harm to him. The bear lowers her head and licks him on the leg. "What the...? I'm not salami, ya know?"

She raises her head and chuffs.

"I got somethin' for ya. Smuggled them out the kitchen." Walter reaches into his backpack and brings out a package of hot dogs.

She grunts. Walter swears it's a happy grunt. He opens the pack and holds one out to her. She gently mouths the hot dog and takes it. Walter's heart is racing from the fear and thrill of the moment. He tosses the rest of the pack away from him. All three bears devour them in seconds.

Walter takes a long drag from a fresh joint. Rizzy tips her head as if inhaling the smoke he just exhaled. She waddles away with a huff. The cubs follow her.

Walter falls into blissful sleep.

***

"You were a hero." Junior is holding Samantha's hand as they walk toward the lake.

She shrugs. "It was just common sense. Hopefully, it'll all work out okay. I don't know how far we can trust Mrs. Badmorn."

"Miss Lana seems sincere. When I first met her, I was sure she was working for gangsters. Heh, instead it was an old hag."

"Her driver, Silas, was scary, though."

"Yeah, I'm glad he's out of here."

"Time will tell. I still think she has something up her sleeve."

"Maybe, but you'll be a full-fledged attorney by then. She won't have a prayer against you."

Samantha blushes and leans against Junior. "You're sweet. I hope so."

They stop at the pedal boats on the shore of Lake Watchawanna. Junior holds Samantha's hand and guides her onto the "angry swan" boat. Samantha gawks at its face and giggles. Junior sits beside her and they peddle together onto the lake to watch the sunset. Junior is comfortable and at ease with her. He thought he was once in love with Amy. This is different. He could talk to Samantha all night. He wasn't in love with Amy; he was in lust. Not to say he isn't sexually attracted to Sammy, but this is poles apart from how he felt with Amy. It's a good feeling. As the sun melts into the horizon, Junior leans in and kisses Samantha. They embrace. He strokes her silky brown hair.

She caresses his cheek with velvety hands. "We should get back."

She's definitely not like Amy. "Okay."

They peddle back to the dock. A grunting, growling noise alarms them. Samantha grabs Junior's leg and whispers, "What is that?"

Junior squints his eyes against the fading light in an effort to spy anything. "Maybe Rizzy bear?"

"There!" Samantha points at one of the other peddle boats. Movement under a canvas on the boat is bobbing up and down like something big eating something.

Samantha pushes Junior. "Find out what it is. I'm scared."

He doesn't want to. Whatever it is might jump out of that boat and eat him...but a guy's gotta do what a guy's gotta do, or he won't get laid. Junior quietly steps out of the angry swan boat, picks up a heavy rock, and approaches the creature. It's grunting faster now. *Oh God, I pray it's not eating a camper. Oh God, oh God...* He grabs a corner of the canvas while holding the rock ready to throw. He rips it away with all his might.

There, in front of him, is a creature eating another creature all right. Kelly is giving Harley a blow job on the boat.

Junior's passion is now totally gone. "Oh my God!" He tosses the canvas back at them.

Harley zips his pants. "Can't we have a bit of romance around here?"

Junior wants to hurl. "That's romance?"

"Yeah, shitwad. Move along."

Samantha jumps off of the boat and runs past the couple. "Come on, Junior," she calls.

They run to the pavilion laughing all the way.

"That was gross." Junior pants.

"No sir, it was romance!" Samantha snickers.

"Well, hello there." Wilson peeks out from under a blanket on top of a picnic table.

The couple jumps.

"Oh, sorry." Junior taps his forehead. "I forgot you like to sleep here."

"Me too!" A tittering woman's voice. Muffy peeks out from under Wilson.

Junior's eyes are wide. "Oh God, it's never ending!"

Samantha laughs. "It must be the full moon."

"Know what? I think I'll just walk you to your cabin." Junior is dizzy from the sight of old folks having sex.

"I think you're right." Samantha smiles and gives him a pinch on his hind end.

One their way back, Kim and Max are standing on the shore fishing. They wave.

Junior calls over his shoulder, "Good luck, and don't go into a boat…just sayin'."

<h1 style="text-align:center">24</h1>

<h2 style="text-align:center">A LATE NIGHT</h2>

A rap on Senior's cabin door startles him from sleep. He rolls over in his bed to check the time. Eleven. Everyone went to bed at ten, and even that is late for the seniors. They had a busy day. Samantha taught pool aerobics and she was tough. *Amazing what you can do with a pool noodle.*

A rap on his door again. Senior shakes the cobwebs from his head and answers the door wearing nothing but his red tartan patterned boxer shorts. It's Lana.

Her cool demeanor slips, and she steps back in surprise. "Oh, I'm sorry. I...I thought you'd be up."

Senior yawns. "I am now, what's up?"

Her eyes pleading. "May I come in?"

Senior was so used to having her as an adversary, he completely forgot his manners. "Oh, oh yeah, come in." He steps aside to allow her entry, grabs a pair of shorts from the arm of a chair, and pulls them on. He picks up a shirt from the floor and sniffs it.

Lana holds one side of her nose closed with her index finger. "You don't have to dress. Please don't put that dirty thing on."

"Okay." Senior tosses the shirt and swipes a pile of clothes from a wooden stool so that Lana could sit. He presents it. "Have a seat."

She brushes debris from the seat and sits. "I want to thank you."

Senior points at himself. "Me? You're the one who put Mrs. Badmorn in her place. I'm relieved it's over. I can barely run this place let alone worrying about her taking it over. I gotta admit I'm surprised I'm trusting you to be our go-between. I mean, you lied about the woods, and I thought you cared, only to brush me aside like old shoes, even though you told my ex-wife I made your toes curl. I just...I just can't get you out of my...my..."

Lana holds up her hand to make him stop. "I didn't lie about that. It was the truth. You did make my toes curl."

Senior straightens with the hope he's not so bad after all building in his chest. "Really?"

"I lied about caring. If I showed any emotion toward you, I would have been fired. I spent my life practicing not caring. I did my best not to give a damn when my clients bought property out from under hard working people." She stands. "I admit it was good money." She approaches Senior. "But I'm tired of living that way. You gave me an out. I'm free. Look." Lana steps back.

Senior regards her. She is more beautiful than ever. She's glowing. "You let your hair down."

"Yes, but it's something else."

"No makeup?"

She places a hand on her hip. "Really?" Annoyance sharp in her voice.

"Uh," *I better get it right this time.*

Lana holds up her arms.

"No leopard bag!" Senior shouts. He's as thrilled as winning a big prize.

Lana claps. "Right, and...?"

Senior points at her head, excited. "No phone!"

They laugh, fall into each other's arms and kiss; long, lingering.

Lana nuzzles his neck. "Wanna make my toes curl again?"

***

The chill in the air makes Walter shiver. Half-asleep, he reaches for a blanket. He feels around for a cover. There is no cover. His eyes snap open. Walter is still sitting in the rocking chair in his chapel in the woods. It's pitch dark and he has no idea how late it is. He shivers. "Dog gone it." As Walter's eyes adjust to the night, he can barely make out the path leading out of the forest. "Damn it to hell, I shoulda put a flashlight in my bag, or at least a damn phone. Cheese and crackers!"

He swings the backpack over one shoulder and makes his way back to camp. "What the hell? No one bothered to look fer me? Some kind of friends they are. Assholes."

Before reaching his cabin, he bangs on the door of Senior's place. He waits, no answer. He bangs on the door again. "Damn it man, wake up!"

Senior opens the door with a sheet wrapped around his waist. He doesn't appear to be a bit sleepy.

"What time is it?"

Senior shrugs, "Two? Three?"

"What the hell is wrong with you people?" Walter begins to nudge past Senior but is blocked. It's pissing him off more. "Son of a …I almost died of hypocondria out there. Not one goal damn soul went lookin' fer me!"

Senior readjusts his cover, "You mean, hypothermia?"

"Whatever you calls it, I was freezin' my balls off!"

"Well, Scottish Bob, your roommate, should have said something. Far as I knew, you were fine." He pauses a beat, studying Walter. "In fact, you look fine to me."

Walter's caterpillar brows square off at each other. His mustache vibrates. "You dumbass, what if it was Mildred out there? It would have given ol' bag Badmorn another excuse to git this dump."

"You are right." A woman's voice behind Senior. Lana peeks over Senior's shoulder, and she's wrapped in a blanket. "The counselors need to do a headcount every night before lights out."

Walter thrusts a shaking finger at her. "I knew it! You were too busy gettin' laid to worry about ol' grumpy Walter." He nods. "Uh huh, I git it." He waves at the couple while huffing away. "Go on, don't mind me. Yer right. I'm not dead yet."

"Walter!" Senior calls out.

Walter keeps walking, ignoring Senior. "Testostrogen fucks everyone up. Thank the lord above, I don't care 'bout that shit anymore," he grumbles.

He slams the door shut at his own cabin and wraps a blanket around himself to warm up. He saunters over to Bob's bed and kicks it.

Scottish Bob sits up, leaning on his elbow. "Walta?" He rubs his eyes. "What time is it?"

"Oh, about," Walter leans toward Bob's face, "Three in the mornin'!"

"Oh." Bob lies down to go back to sleep.

Walter kicks his bed again. "Hey, didn't you notice I was missin'?"

Bob remains in his prone position. "Aye, twas blessed silence. I figured ye was vizitin' wit' ta tree beers."

Walter tilts his head, narrowing his eyes at Bob, his bushy brows almost hiding them. "Three bears...ain't you clever." He thrusts a finger toward the door. "Not till three in the mornin' ya twat!"

Bob nods, eyes drooping for sleep. "Aye, catchin' some winks." He closes them. "Glad ta beers didnae eat yer sorry arse." Seconds later, Bob is snoring.

"Some roommate," Walter grouses and lies on his bed fully clothed wrapped in the blanket. Seconds later, Walter is snoring.

25

Yep, this one was intentionally left blank too.

"Honestly, I'm not sure why it happened, dag nab it," shouted Walter.

26

STAFF MEETING

Senior and Stitch are standing outside the dining hall. Construction equipment rumbles past them to go up the new road toward what once was Caring Souls Adult Center.

"We need to call a meeting with the counselors," Senior says.

Stitch turns an ear toward his boss. "What?"

"I said, we need to call a meeting with the counselors!"

"We're gonna need to call some cow sellers? Why?"

Senior cups his mouth, "Coun..sell..ors! We need to have a meeting."

Stitch straightens and nods enthusiastically, "Oh, yeah." He salutes Senior. "I'm on it, Mr. Darlin'," and runs off.

Senior isn't sure if Stitch heard right this time, but he'll find out soon enough.

Trailing behind the trucks is a gold cart. A large one with three benches. Senior squints against the sun. "What the...?" It's Dingo. He pulls up next to Senior and stops. The cart is white, with a black roof. There is some kind of golf club logo decal on the side.

Dingo smiles wide, throwing an arm over the passenger seat. "Nice, huh?"

Senior's brows knit, "How...?"

"Got it on the camp account. It was a steal of a deal. I had to move on it quick." He strokes the seat, admiring it.

Senior rolls his eyes, "Uh, huh. But of course. Just like our eight-foot Tiki God, Kane, by the pool."

"Hey, everyone loves him. He's our good luck charm."

Senior spreads his arms toward the vehicle, "Why?"

"To transport campers to Badmorn Spa, guy. They ain't gonna walk all the way there." Dingo taps his forehead with an index finger. "Duh."

Man is he annoying. I should have learned my lesson and not share my account with him. I can sense he's going to screw us again. Senior crosses his arms as if to keep his aggravation inside. "The spa won't be finished until next year. Camp is over next week...so...so, duh, to you."

A sly smile creeps over Dingo's face. "Well, Dicky boy, we need it next week fer the wedding."

The word, wedding, punches Senior in the gut. "Wedding?"

Dingo beams, "Yeah, on the last day of camp, when the families come...just like last year. Cool, huh?" He starts the cart back up. "Gotta pick up the missus, chow." He drives away.

"Who?" Senior calls after him, but he's already too far away to hear.

***

Right after breakfast, before the day's activities, Stitch has gathered the employees at a table in a corner of the dining hall. Leigh Ann is adjusting her glasses while staring at an unknown stain on her apron; Samantha is texting on her phone with one hand while holding Junior's hand under the table with the other; Junior is sitting with a sappy happy look on his face while Dingo whispers something into Miss Pat's ear and she giggles. Nurse Idoyou Oyomama is sorting pills and placing them in order into campers' day-of-the-week containers; Chef Fry is explaining his best macaroni and cheese recipe to Tyrone, AKA Stitch, who is visibly drooling. Of course, Walter is there digging in his backpack and grumbling, "This better be quick," fishes out a CBD gummy bear, and pops it into his mouth.

Richard Darling Senior enters the dining hall from his adjacent office and observes the gathering, pleased Stitch understood after all. He waves to the group, "Good morning!"

A muttering of good morning returns.

"As you all know by now, we have a few things to address before our final camp day family picnic next week," Senior smiles. No response. He clears his throat. At least everyone is looking at him. "First of all, how has the head count been going?"

Stitch raises an arm high to be called upon. "It ain't goin' so well. It's been incozignant."

"Incon...what?"

"Inconzignant. First, hey here, then there, an..." Stitch scratches his chin, "Mostly here...but some gotta go there."

"Where?"

"There...before here." Stitch gazes at Senior as if he's dense.

"What he's tryin' to tell you is," Leigh Ann sniffs the stain, then attention back to Senior. "They've been going to each other's cabins, and some of them go...together somewhere." She makes a hand sign with her finger sliding in and out of a circle she made with her other hand.

Senior winces.

Leigh Ann continues, "They don't like the head count. We had to back off."

"It's been a busy year," Stitch nods.

"Oh, God." Senior looks like he just smelled something really bad. His nose and upper lip are actually touching. "Okay," He sighs, "This brings me to the next subject. Who is getting married?"

Silence. The group ogles one another. Confusion on their faces.

"Hello?"

"It's a surprise," Dingo grins like the Chesire cat in Alice in Wonderland.

"If it's Junior, you better tell me right now." Senior stands feet wide as if he's going to punch someone.

"Dad!" Junior releases Samantha's hand.

Walter stands, bracing his fists on a table. He leans toward Junior. "You marryin' my granddaughter?"

"No!" Samantha jumps to her feet. "Grandpa, you would be the first to know!"

Walter plops back into his seat. "Thank you, God. Don't fu...mess with me like that. I'm an old man. You almost gave me a heart attack."

"Then, who is it?" Senior pushes.

"Don't worry about it, man. We got it under control." Dingo holds his wife's hand.

"Oh, really?" Senior smirks, "And is Kim making the cake again?"

"Oh, hell, no," Chef Fry chuckles.

"It's already on order, and we have a caterer coming in. She said Chef can help her."

"Wait, wait, wait," Chef waves his hands. "Will I git paid the same?"

"Oh yeah," Dingo laughs, "Day off, with full pay."

"Now, I can roll wit' that," Chef Fry leans back in his seat, hands behind his head.

"A mystery. This year is gonna rock!" Leigh Ann pumps her fist in the air. It's the most enthusiasm Senior has ever seen in her.

He places his hands on his hips, "Who's pocket is this coming from? I'm not sure I like this."

"An' I told you, don't worry 'bout it. I got it under control," Dingo taps the side of his head with his finger.

"And what about Mrs. Badmorn? What are we going to do about her?"

"Oh," Dingo purses his lips and tips an imaginary hat. "I invited her to the weddin'."

"What?" A cacophony of disagreement from the others.

Dingo waves to everyone to quiet down. "She'll be fine, you'll see."

"I gotta see her ugly ass horse face," Walter grumbles.

Samantha places a hand on Walter's back. "Grandpa, that wasn't very nice. We should give her a chance."

"Hmph."

"Is it going to be your wedding day, Walter?" Senior grins and covers his mouth to keep from laughing. "I know how well you and Bethany get along."

Walter stands, grabs his backpack, and points at Senior. "Now, don't you be talkin' that way at me. Them are fightin' words." He storms out of the hall and mumbles, "Bunch o' sappy ass suckers."

"Can I come?" It's Stitch. He jogs over to Walter, a huge smile of anticipation on his face.

"Rizzy might be there."

Stitch nods, "Uh, huh, I...I know."

"An' her cubs. They can git a tad rambunctious."

A bead of sweat forms on Stitch's forehead. "Uh, huh, maybe I'll be cool 'bout dem if I have a toke or two of the medicinal greens you gots in your bag...sir."

Walter waves, "Come on, it's 'bout time you learn not to be scared of my woods. You haven't seen my chapel yet."

Stitch's eyes dart back and forth. He wrings his hands. "Correct. Sir."

"Glad you're joining him, Stitch," Senior waves and smiles. "This way he won't go missing again."

Walter turns slowly toward Senior narrowing his eyes, "Smart ass."

Senior chuckles and claps his hands. "So, no one knows who the mystery couple is?

Dingo faces the group. "Just me and Harley. He's pre-siding over the ceremony."

"Mr. Blow me?" Leigh Ann giggles.

"It's Mr. Blowme, the e is silent." Senior wonders if Leigh Ann has consumed some of Walter's gummies when he realizes, "Harley?"

"Yeah," Dingo takes a swallow from a bottle of water. "He got ordained online...free!"

There is an audible "Whoa," from the group.

"I even hired a band, some good friends of mine I met in Vegas." Dingo's chest puffs out in pride.

The employees cheer. Senior steps back, "A band?"

Dingo rolls his eyes, "Shit, man, how many times do I got to tell ya not to worry about it? I got it covered. Geez."

Senior's hand instinctively reaches for his lucky penknife in his pocket and rubs it. "Famous last words," he mumbles. Mrs. Badmorn might be done right now, but he knows she's watching their every move, like an eagle waiting patiently for its prey to be separated from its group to strike. One wrong move, and he's done.

***

Walter strolls onto a path through the woods. Stitch stops at the edge. His heart races, his lanky knees knock together. Memories of being horribly lost in the woods when he was a boy floods his mind. He sweats from every pore.

Walter waves to him, "Come on, kid, you can do it."

Stitch clings to a branch. "Sorry, Mr. Evans, I...I can't."

"Just a few feet away is the most inspirin' chapel you'll ever see." Walter points into the woods.

All Stitch can see is trees and more trees. Is that a shadow or a bear? He calls out, "Where's them bears?"

"Not here," A sly smile creeps across Walter's lips, "Yet."

Stitch closes his eyes and prays, "Oh Lawd, oh Lawd."

Walter swings his backpack from his shoulder, unzips it, and bring out a baggy of marijuana. "I got the best stuff here...doctor's orders. I plan on sharing it with the best counselor in these here parts...asides from my granddaughter that it."

"I appreciate it, sir." Stitch wills himself to release the branch.

Walter continues on his way.

Stitch runs to catch up with him. If he loses sight of Mr. Evans, he'll definitely be lost. He grasps the back of Walter's shirt.

Walter swats at Stitch as he walks, "Shit, son, give me some room, will ya?"

Stitch releases him, but hovers his hand mere inches away. A few more minutes of traipsing along a narrow path in the shadowy forest when the sight of open sun-filled space presents itself in front of them—Walter's chapel.

Stitch can finally breath. "Praise the Lawd." It is everything Walter described. He fixed the area up nicely with benches made of tree stumps with wooden planks across their tops. In front of the row of pews is a podium with a rocking chair placed on either side of it. Stitch is in awe. "This your church?"

Walter shakes his head, *no*, while taking a seat on one of the rocking chairs. "It's my chapel."

Stitch nods. "Ah." He has no idea what Walter is talking about.

Walter works at rolling a joint while Stitch retrieves the other rocking chair, pulls it through the leaves, and stops next to him. Walter lights the joint and inhales deeply. He passes it on to Stitch.

Stitch takes a toke, holds his breath, and tries to talk at the same time. His voice only a squeek. "Don't tell nobody 'bout this."

"Heh," Walter takes the joint from Stitch. "They already know. I'm pretty sure they ain't believin' you came into these here woods with me to just to face yer fears—had to be some reward behind it." He inhales from the joint.

Stitch exhales all the smoke from his lungs, and he slumps. "Yeah, you're prolly right."

Walter hands him the joint. "Woo! Bussin' gaslitshit." Fear is melting away with Stitch's high. The sun dappling through the trees is amazing. He holds out his hand to watch the sunlight dance on his skin.

"You only took one hit," Walter raises only one brow. "You ever smoke pot?"

Stitch gazes at the one arched brow, then feels his own in amazement. "Not this, mainly stems an' seeds." He points at Walter's brow. "How you get it up there like that?"

Walter chuckles, "These brows got minds of their own."

"Wowww."

Walter takes a toke. "This here is primo."

Stitch accepts the mostly burned down joint and admires it. "Yeah, primogaslitshit."

Walter agrees, nodding his head in slow motion. "Got some gummies fer ya too."

"Cool."

"Ma!" A distant cry.

Stitch sits up, "Who dat?"

Walter leans forward, "A bear."

Stitch is too relaxed and mellow to worry about it. If Walter runs, then he'll worry about it. "You're playin' me."

"Ma!" A bear cub waddles into the clearing.

Stitch considers it, cocking his head. "Say, Mr. Evans, I think Rizzy shrunk."

"He's one of her cubs."

"Oh," Stitch shuts his eyes, chuckling...until he realizes mama bear must be nearby. He probably should panic. Oh well, I'm sure she's cool.

Soon, Rizzy and her other cub lumbers through the brush into the clearing. Stitch takes an inhale of pot while watching the scene before him. Rizzy approaches and sits on her haunches only feet away. She sniffs at the air, stands and approaches him. He might be high, but this ain't good. He takes a death grip on his rocker and tightly closes his eyes. He doesn't want to see himself shredded to bits. Rizzy nuzzles Stitch's pants pocket.

"You got somethin' in there she wants," Walter chuckles.

Stitch's eyes grow wide. "Oh, my lawd, I put some beef jerky in them in case I got lost."

"Maybe you should give it to her, so she don't mistake yer leg fer beef jerky. Move slow an' steady."

"Oh, Lawd, oh, Lawd let me live...please," Stitch whispers while slowly reaching for his pocket. He's drenched in sweat. His butthole is clenched up to his neck. He slides his hand into his pocket underneath Rizzy's nose. All she would have to do is open her mouth and her huge sharp teeth would crunch his hand right off. He brings out the jerky. Rizzy steps back and jumps up and down on her two front feet. The cubs wrestle unaware of what Mama is doing. Without another thought, Stitch tosses the beef jerky at her. Rizzy lies down with the jerky in her mouth and gnaws on it.

"See that? You made her a happy girl. You just made a friend," Walter's smile seems to be wider that his burly mustache.

Stitch takes a breath, the first one since she approached him. He peed a little in his shorts.

The cubs come to their mother for milk. She leans back as they drink, her eyes half closed in contentment.

"Stitch! Walter! Are you guys in there?" The rustle of leaves and snapping of twigs alarm the bears.

27

ALL HANDS ON DECK!

Rizzy rears up to full length on her hind legs.

Stitch cowers in his chair. "Oh, Lawd, save me. If you let me live, I'll neva' tell anotha' lie...not even a fib, please, Lawd."

Rizzy growls, sniffing the air.

The call is closer. "Hello? Are you folks alright?"

The cubs run for cover. Rizzy lands on all fours, inches from Stitch. He shuts his eyes. His hearing has gone into hypersensitivity. Rizzy's panting, her cubs calling for her, the tromping of leaves of humans approaching, and the chirping of a distant bird. He smells the musk of bear fur mixed with wet leaves and marijuana smoke. Suddenly, it's gone.

Walter's voice, "Over here, goal dang it! What's the hub bub all about?"

Stitch opens his eyes. He's still alive and intact. Relief. "Woo!"

Bethany appears in the chapel clearing along with Senior and Scottish Bob. She pecks at Walter, "You two were gone for hours. We got worried about you, you old coot."

Bob walks over to Stitch. "We saw ta beers. I reckon ye pissed yeself."

Stitch smiles wide and wipes the comment away. "Naw, dog. I was calmlitude the whole time...mellow, ya know?"

Bob chuckles. "Sure, me lad...sure."

"We need to get back." Senior reaches for Walter's bag. "It's going to be dark soon."

Walter slaps Senior's hand. "I got it."

Senior pulls his hand back and glares at Walter like a disciplined toddler. "Fine, I wasn't going to steal your..." He makes quote marks with his fingers. "Prescriptions."

Stitch suddenly finds the comment to be hysterical. "Prescriptions...a hahahaha!" He doubles over with laughter.

Bethany thumbs toward him. "What's wrong with Tyrone?"

"Me thinks tis the prescriptions." Bob winks at Stitch.
***

Back at camp, it is all hands on deck preparing for the surprise wedding. Leigh Ann is in the kitchen helping Chef prepare hors d'oeuvres. She opens a can of Vienna sausages, drains them, then reaches into the fridge for several cans of crescent rolls. She unravels the cover from one and taps the now brown tube onto the edge of the counter. It pops open with a satisfying, POOF. Dough oozes from the opening. She twists the tube to ease the bloating of pre-fabrication, releasing it from its cardboard prison, and places the dough onto a clean cutting board. Pulling it apart along the doughy dotted line, she takes a sausage and rolls it into the crescent.

Chef Fry is sliding a tray of mini pizzas into the oven. "Make sure you use it all. We're gonna have a lot of guests."

Leigh Ann sniffs while pushing up her glasses with a free hand. "Who's making the cake?"

"Someone all the way from Asheville. It'll be here this afternoon."

She pops a sausage into her mouth when Chef isn't looking. "Does it got a topper on it? I can make another one for this year."

Chef Fry's stomach jiggles with his laughter while checking on Gumbo simmering on the stove. "Naw, child, the cake lady is bringin' that too."

Leigh Ann stops rolling sausages to pick stray dough from her fingers. "Does anybody know who's getting married?"

"Mister Harley does, cause he's officiatin' but he won't even tell Miss Kelly who it is."

"I bet it's Muffy again. She's gonna marry that electrocuted wildman, Wilson. She likes to hook up with weirdos."

Chef Fry guffaws with laughter, "Electrocuted wildman...I love it, I'll call him, E.W."

Leigh Ann snorts, "No, it's true. Miss Muffy is into guys who's DNA was in hot pockets and microwaved too long."

Chef Fry sucks in a deep breath from laughter, "Girl, you're gonna be the death of me." He leans against the counter next to Leigh Ann's work. "Ya know, Dingo is really into the prep for this thing. Could he and Miss Pat be plannin' a proppa ceremony? I hear 'bout folks doin' that after a quicky weddin'."

Leigh Ann considers the statement, the dough and wieners untouched. "Maybe."

Chef Fry pulls open the refrigerator and lifts two large catfish fillets from the bottom drawer.

Leigh Ann returns to her work for a brief minute and stops. "I got it, Scottish Bob and Mildred!"

"What?"

"Yeah, I see them together all the time...at the same table for meals, at the pool, on the same pickle ball team..."

"That's crazy." The chef opens the back door.

Leigh Ann peeks over her glasses at Chef. "Oh, yeah? Mildred needs a home, and Bob has one."

Chef Fry steps outside and waves the fish in the air. Rizzy comes lumbering from the edge of the woods. He tosses them toward her. She nods her head up and down before chomping on a fish. She grunts. One of her cubs runs full on toward the other fillet, snatches it, and trots back. Rizzy lies down, relishing her meal.

Leigh Ann thumbs toward the door. "Does Miss Kim know about that?"

Chef Fry places a finger against his lips. "Shh."

Leigh Ann's eyes grow wide, causing her glasses to slip down her nose. "That's it, Miss Kim and Max."

Chef shuts and locks the door. He turns to face Leigh. "Now, you're really talkin' crazy. Mista' Max is one of those non-binary folks."

Leigh Ann shrugs. "How do you know that?"

"He ain't into women...or men."

"I don't think that makes you non-binary. He's a nice guy. So, he doesn't talk about sex like ninety percent of guys."

Chef Fry scratches his head. "Hm, maybe 'cause he don't like sex. I know I wouldn't if'n I had to be Miss Kim's side man."

Leigh Ann covers her ears with doughy hands. "La, la, la, I can't hear you."

Chef smirks. "Or maybe he got turned on watchin' her catch those fish bare handed. Oh, yeah."

Leigh Ann uncovers her ears while glaring at chef. She pushes her glasses back up her nose. "Gross."

28

WHO'S BUYING?

Richard Darling Senior stands on the dock of Lake Watchawanna gazing at the early morning mist lifting from the cooling water. Birds chirp in the distance greeting the sun breaking the horizon. Tomorrow is the last official day of camp. Someone is getting married as well—a surprise wedding. Dingo has opened all the stops for this one. He wasn't at the camp last year when Muffy and Doug got hitched. It was a simple ceremony by the pool under the gaze of eight-foot Tiki God, Kane. The girls made the decorations, the cake, and the topper. The guys built the wedding arbor and decorated Doug's mobility scooter. They played music on a Bluetooth speaker, and everyone had a good time.

Dingo seems to be free with the camp funds for this event. Senior hates any kind of conflict, but he's got to know the numbers for his budget. Obviously, Dingo doesn't have a clue about finances, since his Vegas project went bust so fast. There's something about Dingo that makes Senior want to help the guy out. His boisterous enthusiasm is addictive. It's a refreshing counter to Walter's pessimistic grumbles. Both men are invaluable to the camp, but he's got to get up the nerve to tell Dingo to put on the brakes for his spending.

"What the hell is that?" Walter's voice.

Senior jumps alert from his ruminations. Walter is lumbering toward him while pointing to a white box truck driving along the lane toward Camp Sedation Falls. It doesn't resemble the myriad construction vehicles that have been coming through the past month. It rolls onto the grass and up the hill toward the pool area. The truck parks next to the pavilion. The side of it reads, "Virtuoso Rentals". Two men exit the truck, stroll to the back, open the box gate, and pull out a ramp.

Senior approaches the tall guy dressed in white coveralls. "Hi, can we help you?"

The guy nods. "Yeah. Where do ya want the tent?"

Senior walks up the ramp and checks out what is inside the truck. Not only is there a deconstructed tent inside, but there are also tables and chairs and a flowered wedding arch.

"Hey," Walter shouts from outside the truck, "Check it out."

A florist van is rumbling up the lane. Walter's bushy brows arch for battle and his mustache vibrates.

He grasps Senior's arm, "You better git a handle on this shit...partner."

"Hello?" Coverall guy taps Senior on the shoulder.

"Um..." Senior rubs his lucky penknife. "I guess beside the dining hall."

The coverall guy grins like he just had a good steak, or maybe more like found a new sucker. "Perfect." He shoves a clipboard at Senior. "Sign here."

It's a cool morning, but Senior is sweating profusely while he signs...

"Look!"

A huge tour bus is rolling up the lane. Spots block Senior's sight. He feels about to faint. "Oh, God." He leans over to breathe and reaches out a hand to Walter for support. "Do you know anything about this?"

"Hell no. Your buddy, Dingo, gots a lot of explainin' to do. We ain't gonna pay fer all this shit. I'm tellin' those some o' bitches to turn that damn bus around an..."

"Perfect, they're here." Dingo materializes out of the blue beside the men. "Hey, Dicky, what you all bent over for? You gonna throw up from excitement?"

"You can say that." Senior straightens.

Walter's brows knit hard enough to create their own sweater. "I'm tellin' that goal darn driver to turn his effin bus right around an'..."

Dingo waves his arms into an X. "Whoa, whoa, whoa. Someone's gonna pop a clot. What are you guys all worked up about?"

"You!" Walter steps in front of Dingo, fists balled. All the while the bus is parking. "Where the hell you git off spendin' all our money on this mystery weddin' shit?"

"It's your wedding, isn't it? After all I've done for you. I never should have given you access to our account again." Senior slaps his own forehead. "I'm such an idiot."

Dingo takes a step back. "Yeah, you are." He motions toward the bus. The doors open. "The couple gettin' married is payin' for it, and it ain't me. I didn't charge you for nothin', an' I don't have the money for this shit either."

"What about the golf cart?"

"Yeah, but that was it, I promise."

Four men carrying instruments and one woman leave the bus and wave to Dingo. He waves back, then turns toward Senior and Walter. "Some friends you are. I see how it is."

"I'm sorry." Senior wipes his brow with the back of his hand. "I...I've been under a lot of pressure, you know? With Mrs. Badmorn and all."

"We'll talk later." Dingo moves to greet his guests. "I gotta meet my friends. At least *they* trust me."

As Dingo walks away, Walter mumbles, "Suckers."

The air escapes Senior's lungs, and his muscles relax with relief. It's not his money going to this soiree. He sits on the grass to watch the set up.

Walter joins him. "Someone here must be loaded." His brows separate to arch for the sky. "Confound it, I hope Sammy doesn't ask fer a weddin' like this. Her parents an' I'd have to go wearin' potato sacks and live in a trailer by the river."

Senior playfully punches him in the shoulder. "I'll help you out."

Walter lifts his index finger. "I'll hold ya to that."

By the end of the day, the dining hall and pool area are absolutely stunning. Flowers of all colors occupy every nook and cranny. A willow arch bedecked with

Wisteria is standing in front of Tiki God, Kane, who doesn't seem to mind—his toothy smile forever carved into his face. White folding chairs are set up all around the swimming pool.

Inside the hall, white fairy lights are stretched in several directions across the ceiling. The round tables are covered with white tablecloths. Each one has a multi-colored floral centerpiece. Two six-foot long tables are in the front covered with flowers, candles, and tulle. Next to them is a raised pedestal to place the cake.

Outside, beside the hall, is the band tent with more tables, lights, and flowers. Walter's bar is in the tent with a new varnished countertop. Men are stocking it with crates of beer, wine, and liquor. There is a stage set up at one end with a drum kit and speakers. The band is performing a sound check.

Walter bellies up to the bar for his evening shot of Jim Beam, but a bartender stops him. "Sorry sir, this is for tomorrow."

Walter's mustache shivers, his lips tremble, and his hands ball into fists. "If you want to live long enough to see tomorrow, you sure as hell better pass me that bottle!" He points at the bottle the man is holding.

Dingo intercepts. "Yo, guys, I got it. This one's on me." He winks. "You better hand it over."

The bartender, who's visibly annoyed, holds the bottle of Jim Beam straight-armed toward Walter.

Walter snatches the Beam. "That's better." He unscrews the cap and takes a swig. "Ahhh."

He passes it to Dingo. "Here's to thinkin' before sayin' dumb shit." Dingo takes a swallow and passes the bottle to Senior.

Senior holds it up. "You're right, and I am a dumb ass."

Dingo and Walter nod in agreement.

"But, be sure I get receipts, okay?"

Dingo salutes. "Right away, boss."

"Here's to thinking before opening my big mouth." Senior gulps the Beam and weazes to catch his breath.

The bartender winces. "That's not sanitary."

Walter leans against the bar nose to nose with the man. "An' yer ignant. Liquor kills germs." He leans back and rubs his stomach.

Senior passes the Beam back to Walter, who takes another swig before replacing the cap. He nods to the bartender. "Tell ya what, I'll just take this bottle. I'm sure whoever's throwin' this shindig won't mind."

Dingo puffs up his chest. "Yeah, it's covered, man." He tosses a bill onto the counter.

The bartender plants his hands on top of the bar, "But..."

Walter pats Senior on the back. As the men stroll away, Walter holds up the bottle of Jim Beam and calls over his shoulder, "An' thanks."

29

THE BIG DAY

Families of the campers roll into Sedation Falls for the big wedding. Stitch, wearing a bright orange vest, wildly swings his arms whilst directing drivers to their parking places.

Walter studies everyone being greeted by Senior. Maybe their body language will give away who the bride and groom are. So far, nothing. Leigh Ann and Samantha are acting as ushers, guiding campers and their guests to the seats beside the swimming pool. Everyone is dressed nicely, but no sign of tuxedos or wedding gowns. *If any-one knows who's getting' hitched, it's gotta be ol' Bethany.* Walter stops her on the way to her seat. "Hey."

Bethany blushes as pink as her frilly dress. "Hey, you want to sit with me?"

Walter grimaces. "Maybe later. Who's gettin' hitched? I know you know."

"Oh, you," she giggles, "I promised not to tell...even you. I'm surprised you, of all people, want to know."

"Damn it, woman. I'm just curious." *Why did I even ask?*

"Come sit with me," she insists.

He really doesn't want to. "Okay."

They begin to walk together to a seat when...

"Mom?"

Bethany turns and faces her son. "Kurt?"

The kid's a jerk, but Walter can sense her heart leaping for joy. Bethany's whole face is a smile.

"Hi." Kurt waves.

Last time Walter saw Kurt, the idjet peeled out of the parking lot. His tires spun on the rocks, throwing them against Sammy's car. He doesn't look as cocky as he did that day. He appears...apologetic.

"I missed you, Mom."

"Oh, honey, I missed you too." Bethany embraces her son.

Walter doesn't trust him. He bets the asshole will ask for money or something like that.

She takes Kurt by the arm. "Come sit with me."

Bethany and her son stroll away arm in arm from Walter without a second glance. He's surprised to be a bit disappointed. *I'll sit with Samantha, but I'm gonna keep an eye on that rock throwin' impatient, son-of-a-bitch. He ain't takin' advantage of ostrich-eyed Bethany on my watch. No siree.*

A duet from the band Dingo hired is playing next to Tiki God, Kane. The girl is singing and playing guitar, while one of the guys is on keyboard. They are almost drowned out by Muffy's family on arrival. "Megan, go get Ronnie, he's runnin' for the woods."

Another one of Muffy's daughters grabs the arm of a female tot teetering at the edge of the pool. "No, no." A boy of about ten is standing at the end of the pool and lifts his arms as if he's going to dive. "Get your ass over here, young man. No swimming until after the wedding, you hear me?"

The boy screams and storms to a seat.

Walter is relieved when Muffy arrives to calm the troupe down. He takes a seat behind Bethany to keep an eye on Kurt. He rubs his chin. "Everyone is here. Who the hell is it?"

"I have no idea, Grandpa."

He jumps, unaware Samantha and Junior have taken seats beside him.

Scottish Bob arrives in his full kilt uniform, along with a bagpipe player. Bob has a drum strapped to his shoulders, and the two men stand next to the Wisteria covered arch.

Walter nudges Samantha. "Is it them?"

Junior leans to get a better look. "I don't think so. They look like they're gonna play."

Walter spies Mrs. Badmorn arriving with Lana. "The twat."

Bethany spins in her seat and glowers at Walter.

Walter's caterpillar brows arch like inch worms. "Not you." He points at Mrs. Badmorn. "Her."

Bethany shakes her head. One side of her lip curls down. "God, Walter, let it go. She can't hurt us."

"Oh, yeah? You don't know that." He leans close to Bethany and whispers while thumbing toward Kurt. "He ask fer money yet?"

"No!"

Kurt turns toward Walter. "Sir, I am sorry about last year. I was under a lot of stress. I'll be happy to reimburse you of any damage..."

"Forget it, too late now."

Kurt turns back.

Samantha elbows Walter. "Grandpa, really?" She taps Kurt on the shoulder. "It was MY car, and I forgive you. Water under the bridge."

Walter scoffs, "Yeah, he can't help he got rocks tumblin' between the ears."

Bethany reaches behind herself and swats Walter with her purse.

"Want me to kick his ass?" Tiffany is standing next to Walter, burning a hole in him the size of Texas with her eyes.

"No, he means well." Bethany jabs a finger at Walter. "Keep my son out of your mouth!"

"Next time...and bam!" Tiffany punches the palm of her hand.

Walter leans back in his seat. "Jeez Louise."

Samantha squeezes his right hand while Tiffany moves to take a seat on his left.

"That seat's saved," Walter blurts.

"Oh yeah? For who?"

"Bob, when he's done playin'."

"Yeah, right."

Shit.

Suddenly, he's jabbed in the shoulder. Junior is reaching behind Samantha to do it. "She's here, the queen of mean," Junior hisses. "And her lackey, Lana."

"I know." Walter turns in his seat. Mrs. Badmorn is still dressed head to toe in black. Her face is contorted as if smelling cat piss. Lana is wearing a nice, flowered sundress, and her hair is down. Walter's never seen her like that before. Silky brunette strands fall at her shoulders. She isn't wearing her signature sunglasses and she's smiling. Such a stark contrast to Badmorn. Senior stands at his seat and moves over to give the women their seats. *His damn face is glowin'. What a sappy asshat. I'm glad I'm done with women. Helen was enough. I miss her, but I like my life the way it is. I don't need no bossy woman around to complicate it.*

As if hearing his thoughts, Bethany turns in her seat and winks at him. "I forgive you, Walter bear."

Walter bear? Got damn it, shut yer mouth, woman, is what he wants to say, but instead, cracks a scowl of a smile and nods.

The duet begins to play *At Last* by Etta James. Everyone stands for the bride to arrive under the arch, but Walter can't see the groom. Isn't he supposed to be there to greet the bride?

*At last. My love has come along. My lonely days are over, and life is like a song. Oh, yeah, yeah...*Two minutes into the song and no one has arrived. Guests and campers glance about. Who is it? Maybe it was a stupid joke, but somebody paid for this elaborate getup. The song ends. Walter assumes the Wedding March is next because everyone stands, but instead, the female singer croons, *Wise men say...only fools rush in, but I can't help falling in love with you.* Walter is used to Elvis Presley's voice in this song, but this girl is doing a swell job. *Shall*

I stay? Would it be a sin, if I can't help falling in love with you. Walter leans in toward Bethany's back. "Psst, where are they? Who is it?"

"I'm not saying," is her harsh whisper.

"Fuck it, I'm sittin' down," Walter begins when Max shuffles out of the row he was sitting in. Walter figures it can't be him. He doesn't believe the guy ever had a girlfriend, and he's wearing his usual Camp Sedation Falls outfit. Besides, who could it be? Kim? "Yeah, right."

Max steps under the wedding arch and stands proud. *Like a river flows, surely to the sea. Darling, so it goes...some things are meant to be.*

"What the...?"

Kim shuffles out from her row to rousing applause. Her smile envelopes a lovely face Walter can see since she isn't wearing her hat. Her hair is up in a tidy bun, and a dress made of champaign colored tulle with a tiny pink carnation pattern adorning it frames her figure perfectly. Walter should have picked up on that. Kim never wore a dress at camp. Her children, Jane and Joe, take her by the elbows and walk with her to the arch. *Take my hand. Take my whole life too, for I can't help...falling in love with you.* They release her to join Max, hand in hand. *No, I can't help...falling in love with you.*

Harley steps up into the center of the Wisteria arch and faces the crowd. He is in full riding gear—leather boots, and a black leather vest over a black Harley Davidson T-shirt. He's holding a Bible and clears his throat. The crowd sits down and waits quietly for him to speak. He frantically thumbs through the book, then taps a finger onto a page. "Today, on this magnificent August day we will witness the union of Miss Kimberly Yung to Mr. Maxwell Fisher." He scans the page, turns to another one, turns to another one, then taps on it with his finger, and reads aloud, "This is what the Lord said to me; take from my hand this cup filled with the wine of my wrath and...wait a minute." Harley licks a finger and thumbs to a different page. "Sorry about that." He places his finger on the book. "Okay, here we go." He clears his throat. "So, they are no longer two, but one flesh. Therefore, what God has joined together, let man not separate." Harley looks up. "So..."

Kim gently grasps his wrist. "I have something to say."

Harley smiles, and sighs with relief. "Be my guest."

Kim takes Max's hands into hers. "Da desert and da parched land will rejoice and blossom. Like da crocus, it wheel burst into bloom. Den, will da lame leap like a deer, and da mute tongue shout for joy. Water wheel gush fort in da wilderness and streams in da desert. Gladness and joy wheel overtake them, and sorrow and sighing wheel flee away. Isaiah thirty-five. Dis is how I feel when I'm with you. My parents arranged my first marriage. Dey were afraid I would neva' bear dem grandchildren. I love my children, but I was relieved my husband die young. He was bad side man. You, you are best side man eva." Kim bows her head. "And my best friend, eva."

Max blushes and squeezes Kim's hand. "I believed love and desire were out of reach for me and I accepted it, until June tenth of last year when you plopped yourself on the ground to wait for me to get ready to be your side man. You shocked me, until I realized you meant you needed someone to help haul in your fish. Well, Kim, you hauled me in that day too. I thought about you all year. I couldn't wait to come back to camp, and I prayed you would be here. I will always be your side man."

***

Senior's heart swells watching the ceremony. How fortunate to host two weddings in two years, and he hopes it will become a tradition. This is what inspires him to keep the camp. Something else swells when Lana places her hand on his thigh and strokes it. His heart thumps in his neck. He always knew she wasn't lying when she told his ex he was the best lay she's ever had. He wants to skip the reception and take her straight to bed, but it wouldn't be very gentleman-like.

Walter is glaring at Senior and Lana instead of watching the wedding ceremony. He's squinting so hard; his bushy brows practically cover his eyes. "Gol dang it, worst sappy lovesick puppy eyes I ever saw."

Samantha nudges him. "Grandpa, shush," she whispers.

"She's gonna seduce him into sellin' this place. I know it."

"Grandpa. Relax, please? Let's enjoy the day, okay?" Samantha squeezes his hand.

Walter notices Dingo sitting a few rows behind Senior, and he's glaring at the couple too. Walter nods to Samantha. "Yer right, Sammy. He can't sell without Dingo an' I."

"Shh!"

***

Harley nods to Kim and Max. "You guys got the rings?"

Kim tsks, annoyed. "Of course we do."

Jane hands Kim a ring. She slides it onto Max's ring finger. It's a maple band with interlocking fishhooks embedded in acrylic. "To my always side man."

Kim's son, Joe, hands Max a ring. It is the same style of ring Kim placed on him. Max slides it onto her finger. "To the best catch of my life."

Harley bows. "Till death do you part."

Kim pushes Harley with her right hand. "You be quiet. Sign marriage contract."

"Jeez, alright."

Kim gazes at Max. "You may keese da bride."

Max and Kim kiss on the lips to thunderous applause. Scottish Bob begins drumming while the bagpiper plays, *Amazing Grace.*

"Why the hell is he playin' that?" Walter grouses.

"I don't know." Samantha sighs.

"That song's fer damn funerals."

Bob catches Walters' disapproving glare and shrugs.

30

THE RECEPTION

"Kawa Bunga!" One of Muffy's grandchildren dives into the pool fully clothed.

"Leroy. Get your ass out of that water right now, young man!" Menda shouts.

His little brother, Ronnie, dives in behind him.

"And get Ronnie."

Walter is splashed, and he jumps back. "Git those brats outta there!"

"You callin' my kids brats?"

Menda's younger sister, Megan, is trying to corral the boys, running along the edge of the swimming pool. "C'mon, do what your mother said."

"I call 'em as I see 'em." Walter thrusts a finger toward the pool. "Ain't no control."

"Well, it was stupid to have a wedding ceremony beside a swimming pool in the middle of summer and expect nobody to jump in." She kicks a chair into the pool. "Idiotic."

"Why...why..." Walter sputters, mustache quivering, hands balled into fists.

"I got it." Stitch stands at the shallow end of the pool holding open a towel. "C'mon, guys. Let's dry off an' git somethin' to eat."

"Yeah!" Leroy cheers, "I'm hungry." He wades out to Stitch's towel.

"Me too!" Ronnie wades out to a second towel Stitch hands to him.

The chair, floating near the edge of the pool, is snatched by Megan.

Menda grabs her purse from a chair; her bottom jaw jutting out in defiance and shoots Walter a look that would pierce an alligator's hide. She collars the boys, pulling them along with not a word of thanks to Stitch.

Muffy follows her family toward the reception tent and stops at Stitch. "Thank you, Tyrone. My family can be a bit...headstrong."

"No problem, ma'am." Stitch smiles his usual wide, happy smile.

Walter scoffs, *Hmph, if I had my way, I'd kick the whole lot of 'em out.*

Walter follows the group into the reception tent. Flowers of all colors are draped across the head table set for a dozen members of the bride and groom's family. Bouquets of flowers are centered on round tables covered with white linen. The white party lights strung across the ceiling of the tent create their own constellation of stars. It's all too damn beautiful to Walter. Max or Kim must be loaded. "The cake's probably some six tiered monstrosity," he grumbles, yet he's got to see what gaudy expensive shit it is. *I bet the topper is a cou-*

ple holdin' up a big ass catfish together, he chuckles to himself.

On the cake pedestal is not a tiered cake, but a huge one in the shape of a black bear sleeping. Two smaller cub cakes are placed nearby. They are all covered in a dark chocolate fluffy frosting. Walter is completely taken by surprise. "What the...?"

Kim places a hand on Walter's back. "It's a S'mores cake in hona' of Rizzy an' her pups."

"You mean, cubs, right?" Walter's smile is so wide, his brush of a mustache stretches to keep up.

Kim nods vigorously. "Yes, cubs."

"This is fu...fantastic!"

"We knew you'd like it." Max joins Walter and Kim.

"I don't want you to cut it." Walter is in awe.

"Eats filled wit' marshmallow cream."

Max takes Kim's hand. "And graham crackers."

Drool escapes the corners of Walter's mouth. "Alright, if you must."

Scottish Bob approaches and gawks at the cake. "Innit a barry braw cakey."

"Yeah, it is." Walter slaps Bob in the arm with the back of his hand. "What the hell was that? That song ya played? It ain't fer weddin's."

"Amazin' Grace is ta only one Cedric knows."

Walter shakes his head, chuckling, his mood lightening up.

"There you are." Tiffany grabs Scottish Bob's arm. "Come sit with us."

She pulls Bob away as he mouths, *save me* at Walter.

Walter smiles and waves. He moves toward the cake Kim and Max are beginning to slice, when he is cut off by a pair of big ol' ostrich eyes.

Bethany's head bobs. "Come dance with me." She snatches Walter's hand.

He tugs it away. "There ain't no music."

The band begins to play, *Walking on Sunshine* by Katrina and the Waves.

"I can't dance. Go find another sucka'...uh, friend to dance with."

Samantha and Junior stroll up to him. "Oh, Grandpa, go dance with her." They're holding hands. Walter squinches one eye at Junior and growls.

Samantha stomps her foot and slaps her leg. "Grandpa, really?"

"Jus' makin' sure the boy don't try any funny business."

"Sir, you know I'm a straight up guy."

"That's the problem...yer straight."

"Walter!" Bethany slaps him in the arm.

"And don't it feel good, hey!" Junior sings along with the band.

Walter chuffs.

"Go dance with her, Grandpa. It won't kill you, you know?" Samantha and Junior move toward the dance floor.

Walter points at Junior. "Lookit him, he dances like a squirrel with his nuts caught inna chain-link fence."

Bethany doesn't answer. She only glares at him.

After a moment of awkward silence... "Fine, if I dance, will ya leave me alone?"

Bethany nods, takes both of Walter's hands, and begins to guide him to the dance floor when...

"Ayeiii! Ha, ha, ha!"

"You got marshmallow cream and graham crackers in your hair!"

"Ha, ha, now you do too!"

Walter's caterpillar brows arch to the sky and vibrate in panic. "The cake!"

Bethany runs with Walter to the bear-cake table. Max and Kim are in a full out cake fight. Rizzy cake is now only a pile of chocolate, marshmallow cream, and graham cracker crumbs. Kim smooshes Max's face with a big handful of it. Walter lunges for the plate topped with a cub cake, snatching it away from harm's way. Bethany grabs the other one, and they carry them to a safe table. Her quick action makes Walter almost like ol' ostrich eyes.

"Look out!"

A glob of cake hits Walter on the side of his face. He braces himself in front of the cub cakes. "Protect the cubs!"

Bethany buttresses herself next to Walter. Remains of Rizzy cake flies in all directions. A gob of marshmallow slaps Bethany in the chest. A whip of chocolate slaps Walter on the mustache, but he and Bethany stand firm.

Muffy and Wilson rub chunks of s'mores cake over each other. They begin making out and licking frosting from one another.

Walter shuts his eyes tight from the scene of such carnage. He hears Stitch cry out, "Stop this madness!"

A moment later, it's Kim's voice. "My weddin' cake!"

Walter opens his eyes. Kim is covered in chocolate, marshmallow cream, and graham cracker crumbs. Her hands are stroking her dark hair back. Her lower lip quivers. "We go crazy. Now, no cake to eat."

Walter and Bethany step aside. The cub cakes are untouched behind them. Everyone cheers. Walter turns to shake Bethany's hand. "Good jo..." She grabs him and hugs him. He gingerly pats her on the back. It's actually a pretty good feeling. He's smiling.

Bethany's hand sticks to Walter's shirt when she steps back. "Oopsy, must be marshmallow cream."

Walter's smile is unwavering. "Eh, I'm sticky from flyin' cake anyways."

"I'm cuttin' de cake dis time," says Nurse Oyomama wielding a cake knife. Everyone steps aside for her as she cuts, and Samantha plates the pieces. The scene is much more civilized. The bride and groom are served first, and everyone else gets into a nice, polite line—many of whom have s'mores cake remains on their clothes, faces, and hair. Muffy's grandchildren press their sticky hands on each other, laughing at the goo left behind. "I'm too sticky, Mom." Ronnie reaches for his mother's hand, and she deftly lifts it out of his reach.

"You'll be fine."

"Naw, huh."

Leroy, whispers in his ear. Ronnie shouts, "Kawa Bunga!" and runs out of line to join his brother at the pool.

Menda rolls her eyes. "Tsk, boys."

Their little sister, Maya, pulls on her mother's dress, getting her hand stuck to it. "Me too, Mama."

Samantha glances up from her serving duty. "Somebody needs to go watch them."

Stitch sidles next to her. "I'll do this. You go on ahead an' babysit those raptorsugarats."

"Shh!" Samantha wipes her hands on her pants.

Walter is relieved there is no reaction from the Tyrannosaurus mother.

Samantha takes Maya's sticky hand, and rushes toward the swimming pool.

Walter can sense the collective sigh of relief from the guests, including Menda.

"My mother would have never let me behave that way. What's wrong with kids these days?" huffs Bethany.

Walter smiles...again.

31

MAY THE MOUSE NE'ER LEAVE YOUR GURNAL

The morning after the wedding celebration, campers gather their luggage and families and say goodbye until next year.

Max and Kim wave goodbye from a limo Jane and Joe rented for the couple. They'll be honeymooning in the Smokey Mountains somewhere near Dollywood. Dingo sits forlorn in the driver's seat of his three row golf cart. He had decorated it with streamers and tied empty beer cans to the back. A hand scrawled *Just Married* sign on poster board is taped to the back of the roof.

Muffy approaches him with her three grandchildren in tow. "Why don't you give these children a ride around the grounds before we head home?"

Dingo perks up and sits straight, popping his next to last button on his Hawaiian shirt. He immediately holds it closed. "Sure, sure. We'll take a ride up the road an' check out how much is done at old lady Badmorn's haunted castle."

The children cheer, "Yeah!"

Muffy smiles. "Tell you what. I have a spare T-shirt here. Why don't you put it on and I'll sew the buttons back onto your shirt for doing us this favor?"

"Okay." Dingo removes his shirt and takes the Camp Sedation Falls tee that Muffy hands him. It's obviously three sizes too small, but he pulls it on anyways. It is so tight, the hem rolls up from his stomach and rests against his ribs like a crop top.

Leroy points and laughs. Ronnie and Maya giggle.

Dingo tosses his shirt to Muffy for repairs and keeps the T-shirt on. "Glad you kids like this outfit."

They nod, laugh, and buckle themselves into their seats on the cart. Maya is sitting beside Dingo and the boys have taken the back seat. "This is fun." Maya claps. Dingo drives the golf cart up the paved road toward Mrs. Badmorn's property.

Stitch is loaded up with Bethany and Tiffany's luggage. All Walter can see is Tyrone's spindly legs. Bethany approaches him. "Be sure to thank Senior for us. We had a most fantastic time."

"Where's your son, Kurt?"

"Oh, he had to work today, but he plans to spend much more time with me. He even asked me to move in with him. I told him I couldn't. I'm used to my privacy now."

"Huh, doesn't his wife hate you?"

"Oh, yes, but they got divorced this year."

Walter wants to ask her if it's because the guy's a pain in the ass, but he doesn't feel like getting swatted with her purse again. He spies a clump of marshmallow cream in her hair. He reaches for it, pulls it out between his thumb and index finger, and now they're sticky. Bethany tilts her face up toward his. *She better not try to kiss me.* She hugs him in a tight squeeze instead and kisses his cheek. Walter's mustache quivers involuntarily. *Damn it, the temperature seems to have gone up twenty degrees all of a sudden.*

"And thank you, Walter, for being a not such a bad guy." Bethany releases her grip and winks.

Walter bumbles, his mouth isn't moving the way he wants. It's talking gibberish. "Sure, sure, no problem. Now, go away."

Mildred approaches pulling a rolling suitcase. Tiffany picks it up and tosses it into her trunk like throwing a bag into the garbage.

Mildred's hands go to her hips, and she frowns. "What if you broke something in there?"

Tiffany brushes the comment off. "It's fine."

Bethany takes Mildred by the arm. "Mildred's going to live with us. It's going to be just like the Golden Girls."

Mildred nods vigorously. "Yes."

One corner of Walter's upper lip rises. It's not much of a smile. "Great. Glad fer you, Mildred. Be sure the bathroom is close to yer bedroom. Don't want ya wanderin' off."

Scottish Bob strolls up carrying a duffle bag and his drum. He bows to Walter and the women.

"May de best you've eva' seen
Be de worst ye'll eva' see,
May de mouse ne'er leave your girnal
Wit' a tear drop in its eye,

May yer lum keep blithely reekin'
Til ye're auld enough ta die.
May ye eye be just as happy
As I wish ye now ta be."

Bethany claps her hands; a beaming smile engulfs her face. "How lovely. Thank you, Bob."

Bob puts down his duffle bag to shake hands with Walter. "Ye did good, my friend."

"Thank you. Good poem. Is it a clan sayin'?"

"Naw, got it on Google."

Tiffany hugs Scottish Bob from behind, startling him. "Thank you, we had so much fun."

Bethany nods. "And drama."

Bob turns to face Tiffany. "Ye should be thankin' Walta' here. I'm only a campa'."

Tiffany squeezes Bob's cheeks between her fingers. "Oh, you are modest." She takes her bag from a relieved Stitch. "You'll be here next year, right?"

Bob bites his lip and gives Walter a glance that says, *Uh oh.* "Aye, I plan ta be...kilt an' all."

"Oh yes, definitely wear your kilt. You look so adorable in it."

Bob salutes. "Aye, aye."

She and Bethany wave as they get into Tiffany's car. "Ta ta!"

"Drive safe." Walter grouses.

"No worries." Bethany cheers.

Walter squints his eyes against the sun as Tiffany swerves away. "Hmph, I'll have to call Bethany later to make sure she's home safe."

Bob's mouth turns up into a sly grin. He winks. "O' course ye be."

"It ain't nothin' like that."

Bob picks up his bag and waves. "Doncha let ol' Mistress Badmorn git ye."

"She ain't got a chance in hell. See ya next year." *She better not fuck with Walter Evans. That bird'll lose a lot more than just her nest egg. She'll lose a whole carton of 'em.* Walter wipes his hands on his pants as though wiping dirt from them.

***

Dingo stops the golf cart in front of Mrs. Badmorn's new hotel. The frame is up already and it's huge. The spa, Dingo assumes, is in the middle of the building with a wing of rooms on either side of it. The double roofs are slanted to resemble a bird in flight. The windows have been installed, but there is no siding or shingles on the building yet.

The children ogle. "Is it really a haunted house?" Leroy asks.

"Oh yeah. So, never go near it, or Witch Badmorn will git ya, and have ya for dinner."

"Aren't haunted houses s'posed to be old?"

Dingo raises a finger. "Oh, but there was an old one in that very spot. Mr. Badmorn died in it and his ghost walked the halls. Mrs. Badmorn burned it down to rid it of his ghost, but he remains and haunts the new house." Dingo swings his arm in front of Maya as if to protect her. "Look...there. Do you see him? He just walked past the window."

Maya screams.

Leroy leans in his seat to get a better look. "Yeah, he's all white an' stuff."

"I'm scared," cries Ronnie.

"Okay, okay, tour's over. We better head back." Dingo made the whole thing up, yet the place creeps him out. It's got a weird vibe he can't put his finger on.

***

Back at Sedation Falls, Muffy hands Dingo his shirt and all of the buttons button. They don't all match, but he doesn't care. "Thanks."

Leroy jumps off of the cart. "It was cool. We were scared."

"Scared?" Menda appears to be getting fired up again. Her face is turning red.

"It was a haunted house." Ronnie runs to hug his mother's legs.

"No, no, I was just showin' 'em Mrs. Badmorn's new place. I was jokin'. Kids like scary stuff," Dingo says.

Menda gives him the side eye. "Hmm." And moves on to her van to load up her family.

Muffy nods. "Thanks again. We'll see you next year?"

"Oh yeah, they can't function without me." Dingo starts the cart back up. "See ya next year." He drives on toward the cabins, the cans tied to the back banging and clanking against the gravel drive as he goes.

***

Walter is now alone. All of the campers have left. Stitch is cleaning up the cabins, Chef and Leigh Ann are closing the kitchen, and Nurse Oyomama, Junior, and Samantha are in his office finishing paperwork. It's peaceful by Lake Watchawanna. Walter is tired, but it's a good tired, like he dug all the way to Timbuktu and found gold. This place is his gold, and he'll keep it one more day, and one more day, and one more day, till old Badmorn concedes. Senior has been nowhere in sight. *He said he was going to take Lana home from the wedding right before the cake fight last night. That idjet, what a sap.*

Walter moseys toward the swimming pool. The water is crystal clear...sparkling. Stitch did a good job maintaining it. *I bet it'll feel good.* Tiki God Kane stands at the deep end smiling a toothy grin as if saying, "Oh, yeah." Walter can't resist. He removes his shirt, and begins to unzip his shorts when...

"Hello?"

A woman's voice. Walter glances about. *Where the hell did that come from?*

"Somebody out there?"

"What?" Walter shouts, confused.

"I'm stuck. I can't get out."

32

I'M NOT DONE WITH YOU

*S*he sounds like...no, it can't be.

"Help, get me out of here!"

Walter follows the shouts to the pool bathhouse. He leans an ear against the door. "Is that you, Badmorn?"

"Yes! Get in here. I'm stuck in one of the stalls."

Walter's squirrel tail brows pop up in surprise. He enters the bathhouse.

Mrs. Badmorn bangs on a stall door. "This one. I'm in this one!"

Walter tries the familiar door. It's jammed, all right. *Damn, if it isn't the one Mildred got stuck in. I thought Tyrone an' I fixed it.*

"Open this door, or...or I'm going to sue you to kingdom come."

He jiggles the handle. "Cool yer jets."

"I spent the whole night in here!"

"Doncha got a cell phone in there with ya?"

"It's not working in here."

"You coulda crawled under the door."

"Excuse me? In this filth?"

"Oh yeah, you woulda got stuck there too."

"You son of a…let me out!"

"I gotta call backup. Hold onto yer panties, woman." Walter pulls his cell phone from a pocket to call Stitch, but there is no signal. "Well, I'll be damned, no service."

"See? I told you."

Walter steps outside waving his phone around for a signal. It's good on the deck by the pool.

"Hello?" Stitch answers.

"Hey, Badmorn's stuck in the stall."

"Dang! Strike me pink. Be right there, boss."

Walter pockets his phone and sighs. "Too bad we can't jus' leave her in there."

He saunters back and calls through the stall door, "He's on his way. How come you're in there in the first place?"

"Tsk, I didn't want to be near that cake fight, and…and I wanted to go in peace. All right?"

"Heh." Walter actually does get it. He can't stand public restrooms. "Shoulda been here last year. We had to use outhouses. Talk about not bein' able to go in peace."

"Disgusting."

Walter puts his shirt back on and not even three minutes later, Stitch arrives on the scene, toolbelt wrapped around his hips. He lifts from it a screwdriver and holds it high. "Let's save the enemy from certain death, for we have mercy on even the most vituperative among us."

"Damn, I think that's a real word."

Stitch's skinny chest puffs out with pride. "Yep, I looked it up. Fits Mrs. Badmorn to a tee."

One of Walter's brows dip in thought. "Huh."

"For God's sake, get me out of here!"

Walter steps aside for Stitch to remove the screws to the door and both men lift it out.

Mrs. Badmorn is sitting on the toilet in her black mourning dress, purse in her lap. Her hair is disheveled, and sweat has leaked makeup away from her pasty white face. She is gripping a large wad of toilet paper, and dabs at her neck with it. Shredded bits of paper stick to the bodice of her dress. She stands, taking a breath as though she has been suffocating. "Thank God!" She drops her wad of toilet paper and pushes past Stitch to get to the sink. She turns on the faucet and presses her mouth to the stream of fresh cool moisture. After several good gulps and a splash on her face, she straightens. "I was this close to drinking nasty toilet water."

Walter grins at the thought.

Stitch takes her by the elbow and guides Mrs. Badmorn outside. Her eyes blink at the blinding sunlight. "I want you to know, Mr. Evans, that I am not done with you."

Walter pishes and waves her off, but his gut sinks at the comment. He leans toward her. "Oh yeah? Let 'er rip, tater chip."

"I have no intention of sharing MY guests with your camp. My spa retreat will be ten times better than your "rustic" acres. I guarantee I'll be as big as the Goodnights when you file bankruptcy. I'll be right here to take it and all of this property, and Rizzy.

Steam rises to Walter's head and blows out of his mouth. He thrusts a finger at her. "You keep Rizzy outta this!"

Mrs. Badmorn hisses. "Those woods will be mine."

He's full on fire now. One of Walter's eyes close from sparks flying out at the old battle-ax. "Why you…" he sputters.

Stitch steps between them, arms outreached. "Now, now, you two. Mercy, remember?"

Walter takes a long step back, wrenching his neck in a circle, causing it to make all kinds of cracking noise. "Damn, I thought I'd never miss Merl an' his crazy wife, but I sure as hell do now."

Mrs. Badmorn brushes bits of TP from her bodice, "Oh, the previous owner of Caring Souls? Yeah, he was even dumber than you. He sold us that place for a song. I knew its true value." She pulls her cell phone from her purse and studies the screen. "Tsk, it's almost dead. Call Lana to come and pick me up."

Stitch brings his phone out from the toolbelt and glances up at Walter, who's shaking his head, *no.*

Mrs. Badmorn thrusts her phone back into her purse. "Really? How petty."

The men stand staring at her. Walter's mustache quivers with hankering to fight her, but Walter ain't gonna fight no woman.

"Fine, then." Mrs. Badmorn spins on her heel and marches toward the road leading to her new hotel.

***

The woods abut the lane to Mrs. Badmorn's property. The construction of her spa/hotel is well underway. The framing is complete, and drywall will be installed before the winter hits. She'll have it finished by next summer; in time to snare guests away from Sedation Falls. She'll call it The Instead. As she walks, the woods make her nervous. Anything could jump out at her. "There's too much wildlife around here. I'll have to fix that. Where is Lana?" she says aloud while bringing her phone from her purse. She studies the screen—there is a little reception and ten percent of battery life remaining. It's enough for a phone call. She taps Lana's number.

Ring ring. Ring ring...

She glances up. Rizzy is standing in the road in front of her. She waves a hand at the bear. "Shoo, shoo!"

Rizzy roars, showing her teeth.

Mrs. Badmorn screams, drops her phone, and turns to run, but Rizzy's cubs are on either side of her. She swings her purse at the closest one. He bats it away playfully. Contents of her bag fly in all directions. The other bear licks at an open tube of lipstick, getting red all over its tongue and mouth. *Ma!* The bear rubs at her muzzle with a paw.

Mrs. Badmorn puts her hands together in prayer. "Please, please let me live. I didn't mean it. I...I'll leave you alone. I promise."

Rizzy agitates her head back and forth fiercely. Her whole body shakes and sways like a dog clearing water from its fur.

Mrs. Badmorn murmurs in prayer.

The male cub snatches Mrs. Badmorn's cell phone from the ground and runs into the woods with it, the female cub close behind. Rizzy glares at her. Mrs. Badmorn remembers hearing somewhere that if you make your-self big and yell, black bears will go away. She stands tall, waving her black dress and screams, "Ya, ya, ya, ya!"

Rizzy huffs and runs away from the crazy human in shiny black fur. Her cubs quickly follow.

Mrs. Badmorn takes a deep cleansing breath and bends down to pick up her purse and its contents, but her phone is missing.

***

Richard Darling Senior and Lana are nude and supine in bed at his cabin. Senior has Lana's head cradled on his arm. "I think that was the best night of my life." He strokes her arm.

"Me too," she hums, sleepy eyed.

"I feel a bit guilty for not being out there to see the campers off, but I didn't want this moment to end."

"I'm sure your staff managed it fine."

"Yeah, but Walter will give me an earful anyways."

Double, double, toil and trouble. Lana's phone is ring-ing on the side table. *Fire burn and cauldron bubble.*

Senior moves his arm from under Lana. "Whoa, some ringtone."

"Sigh, it's Mrs. Badmorn. I have a special ringtone for her." *Eye of newt, and toe of frog, wool of bat, and tongue of dog.* "She told me she would take an Uber when we left early. I hope she made it home okay."

Double, double, toil and trouble... "Believe me, that woman can take care of herself."

Fire burn, and cauldron bubble... "I better get that." Lana leans over and picks up her phone. "Hello?" She listens, brows knitted. "Hello?" She puts the phone on speaker. "It sounds like water gushing, some slushing? Is that chewing I hear?"

Senior turns his head with an ear toward the phone, "I think she butt-dialed you. Sounds like she's a sloppy eater."

"You know? She never ate when I was around. I hear why." Suddenly the noise stops. "She must have hung up." Lana leans over and gives Senior a big wet kiss.

***

In the woods, the cub drops the phone it was chewing and steps on it before joining his mother toward Walter's chapel. Their sensitive noses catch the scent of marijuana burning, and that means a treat of "hot dogs"...and maybe a marshmallow or two.

The End...for now.